A Summer Taken

Book One • Council of Friends

by

Jason Milgram

**Dedicated to Christina
and all the other children killed
by guns in the United States.**

JASON MILGRAM

I nodded. If by practically eating nothing the last two years was considered vegetarian, then sure. I hoped Mom had filled Ms. Caroline in on my eating disorder the last two years also, how I'd struggled with keeping anything over 500 calories a day down. If I couldn't control circumstances in my life, then I sure as hell tried by limiting food.

Therapy had helped. I hadn't needed to go to one of those immersive hospitals where they take you away for a month, not that there was anything wrong with that. I was just proud of the fact I'd dealt with it without the extreme intervention. I guess I had my parents to thank for that for being as nosy as they were.

"Well, here it is," Ms. Caroline said, gesturing to the grand expanse of Camp Auctus. It really was a beautiful place filled with caring adults and traditional camp activities, with a heavy dose of social studies thrown in, but seeing it made my heart hurt.

A hot breeze whipped through the courtyard. Pine trees rustled, sending needles raining to the ground. None of what happened that summer two years ago was Camp Auctus' fault. Let's just clear that up right now. But memories don't care whose fault it is. When I was twelve, all that mattered was ice cream with sprinkles in the mess hall after dinner, races past the row of pines, conversation by the lake, archery lessons, arts and crafts, and rainbow sunburst rubber-band bracelets.

That was before it all came to an abrupt end.

Before my world literally shattered.

Being here again hurt—it all reminded me of her.

I settled into my home for the next two weeks—Cabin Infremo—same as my mother's twenty-seven years ago. One of the girls who'd been here since the start of summer ended up leaving when her brother surprise-visited home from the military, so her parents came to pick her up early. Ms. Caroline gave me her spot. I could've just as easily slept alone in the Writer's Hut. I wasn't very good with friendships. In fact, I didn't attend Camp Auctus two years ago at the insistence of my mother, who swore it changed her life—I attended because Elizabeth Richards had single-handedly convinced me to come.

For the first two days, I did the camp thing. That's what she would've wanted me to do. I did the archery, watched the skit performances, applauded the songs, ran the miles, listened to the lessons on our economy, smiled for the cameras, and yes, even had the ice cream with sprinkles. At night, around the campfire, I listened to the stories of Camp Auctus's old days, roasted marshmallows, sang along to both modern and traditional songs, and tried so hard to blend into the painting. It was a beautiful camp, no doubt about that, with caring leadership, gifted campers, all wrapped into a classic lakeside package.

But I still felt like an outsider looking in.

For one reason or another, I had never fit in.

Apparently, Ms. Caroline had talked to the girls about giving me space, because nobody asked direct questions. Everyone sort of acted like my being there was no big deal. I appreciated that more than they realized, because I wasn't thrust into the awkward position of having to explain myself. I also wasn't

TWO

A long, lonely creak welcomed me. I stepped into the mustiness.

The hut smelled stale and humid, like old wood and fresh pine needles rolled into one. The needles littered the edges and corners of the hut, as though insulating the room from the outside world. The scents transported me immediately.

The hut had a big side window, gritty and crusty on the outside with tree dust, a new mini fridge in the corner (was it for me?), a wood-burning stove, and one lantern hanging from a ceiling beam. The highlight of the room, though, was the computer built into the wooden desk that faced a wall graced with a framed painting of the American flag. The computer was made to look like a vintage typewriter, except it was outfitted with AI.

That's where I sat two years ago, writing the book that was going to be my bestselling novel, the first ever published by a twelve-year-old, the one about two best friends becoming sisters by the end of summer. I called it *Lost and Reborn*. I'd be famous! Or so went my silly dreams. I'd gotten about forty pages done and felt incredibly professional and accomplished about it.

I never finished.

Slowly, I walked to the desk chair and placed my hands on its sanded-down frame. It was meant to look rustic, like tree branches fashioned into thin logs before ending up as a sturdy seat. It'd probably been here forever. Some of the women who worked here now had been campers a long time ago, like Ms. Caroline, Ms. Susan, and Ms. Daisy long before my time. The history and tradition rooted in Camp Auctus was hard to ignore—and intimidating as hell.

"Hello, Julia. Welcome back." The computer's screen lit up, the part supposed to look like a sheet of paper in the vintage typewriter.

"Hello, computer."

"Are you here to write again? Another novel? A poem, perhaps?"

"No, thanks. Silent," I instructed it to shut down, so I could think without distraction.

The chair reverberated a deep rumbling sound when I slid it out from under the desk, friction of solid wood against wood. A brown cushion was tied to the seat, three of its four buttons were missing, and it shifted when I sat. I stared at the flag painting on the wall, just like I had two years ago when I'd heard the soft creak of the door opening.

"Hey. I knew you'd be in here."

"Hi," I mumbled. "Of course you did."

I hadn't looked at her. I was still mad that she was leaving when we were only halfway through camp. How was I supposed to get through summer without her?

Closing my eyes, I tried to block out the memory. The silence in the Writer's Hut could be deafening, the isolation and stillness, as campers

14

cheered and screamed in the distance. It was enough to put me in a daze, make my recollections fly right open like loose gates before a storm. Speaking of which...I stood and moved to the door which swayed in the breeze. The sweet scent of rain filled the air.

It had also been a rainy day when I last saw her smile.

Heard her voice.

I'd stared at photos of her a thousand times since she left, but it'd never been the same. I never wrote again after that. In my journal, sure, but not creative writing, not the kind that stirred my soul. Ms. Caroline didn't know, or she wouldn't have asked me to prepare some "nice words" about Elizabeth. Couldn't they have dedicated the new garden while I was gone? Two years was a long time to wait after someone's death. Mom said it was because the camp administrators wanted me here.

I sighed, reached over to the stack of writing paper, blank and half-used composition books, and picked up a purple pen from a cup holding an assortment of pens and pencils. I'd never been fond of my own handwriting and preferred to use a computer instead, but Ms. Caroline insisted we do it the "old-fashioned way." Something about words coming out more organically when you actually formed them with your hand.

The paper felt old-school under my hand. I clicked open the pen and slowly wrote ELIZABETH, underlining her name twice. Next to it, I wrote the date—August 4, 2041. That was as far as I got. The pen ran out of ink.

"Really?" I tossed the empty pen into the trash, found the other pens in the cup to be dried out, and opened the drawer to find another one. Rummaging through, I searched for a good ballpoint. I hated felt tip and those skinny needle-like tips, too. They always cut through the paper.

What my fingers found instead stopped me.

Way in the back of the drawer was a pink envelope. Written on it: JULIA.

With shaky hands, I pulled it forward past the dusty old pencils, loose staples, and paper clips. I brushed off loose debris and blinked a few times. I wasn't going crazy. The envelope said my name in my cousin's handwriting. I'd know it anywhere. Flipping it over, I saw it was sealed.

How did this get here? Maybe it hadn't been her—maybe someone else had written this to me. What if it was meant for a completely different Julia? But it wasn't. I knew it wasn't, because this was Elizabeth's handwriting, all loopy and curly with a little heart dotting the "i."

The envelope quivered in my hands. I tossed it onto the desk like it'd bitten me.

I couldn't read it.

But I understood now. She'd brought this to me on the day she left. She knew I was mad at her for going, so she'd written me a letter, here in the Writer's Hut. It'd been sitting here, waiting out the last two years for me to see it. The Writer's Hut may as well have been called the Dusty Isolation Hut—that was how much other girls my age didn't enjoy being here. Sadly, the Writer's Hut was a relic of the past.

I couldn't bring myself to open the pink envelope. It'd be like taking a knife and slicing the wound open all over again after it'd started to heal. Instead, I fell into the chair, dropped my head onto the desk, and sobbed for what felt like forever.

The alarming sounds of shouts and mass retreat echoed through my head. For a moment, I thought I was there—at the rally. I dreamt of red, white, and blue banners all falling to the ground. I kept worrying I'd see Elizabeth lying on the floor on her stomach. Suddenly, I realized I was never physically there at all, so it wasn't possible.

I was—

Dreaming.

The shouts were actually campers running for cover from the pouring rain outside, and I had fallen asleep at the desk. The computer clock said 6:18 PM. Between the exhaustion of travel and the stress of being back in this place, I'd cried myself to sleep. The rain began falling in sheets outside, as a cool wind swirled into the little cabin from the door that'd blown open.

I saw it again—the pink envelope.

My god, this camp really was haunted. Inside this folded square paper glued shut with Lizzie's DNA was a message, one I couldn't bear to read. With my fingertip, I smoothed the edges, felt the seal, the thickness of its contents, as though I could determine the envelope's severity just from weighing it.

JULIA...

At the ajar door came a knock. I jumped out of my skin and unevenly got up to answer. Ms. Caroline burst in, shaking her umbrella on the little porch, throwing back her poncho hoodie.

"You don't have to knock, you know," I told her.

"I always mind my manners, dear. Rain doesn't change that," she replied, shaking out her wet, fluffy sponge of short gray hair. Her tiny frame invaded the cabin, placed a picnic basket on the desk, and removed the poncho, hanging it over the back of the chair to dry. "I thought you'd be here."

I knew you'd be here, Elizabeth had also said.

"Where else would I be?" I reached behind her for the envelope addressed to twelve-year-old me and slid it into my pocket. "I'm not real friends with anyone here, and I've seen the looks they give me." Negative attention was still special attention.

She waved me away. "Don't pay them any mind. If I'd listened to every girl who'd ever tried to intimidate me in life, I'd still be hiding in a closet somewhere." She looked at me with her calming brown eyes. "You got that?"

"I guess." I plopped onto the dusty couch and stared out the window at the waterfalls cascading over the edge of the roof. Unsealed edges of the window whistled from the wind.

"Oh, Julia."

"What?"

"I can hear it in your voice." From the picnic basket, she pulled out a plastic box, a thermos, and two mugs. She unscrewed the thermos and poured hot chocolatey liquid into one cup. Ms. Caroline's gaze caught mine.

"Hear what?"

"The disdain. I've asked too much of you. I asked your mother if it was alright for you to speak at the Summer's End Show, and she assured me you would enjoy it very much, but I can see I've burdened you. Hot cocoa?"

"No, thanks."

She raised an eyebrow. "I know you're wrestling with demons in here."

"Wrestling...demons?"

"Fighting with yourself, struggling over something."

I thought that was a cool description I could use one day. If I ever got back to writing stories. *Wrestling demons.* "Then I guess wrestling demons is normal for me."

She pursed her lips together in a sympathetic smirk. "I'm sorry, Julia. This is my fault, asking you to come."

I shrugged. "I just never get a say in what I do, Ms. Caroline. You know my mom. She schedules stuff for me without asking how I feel about it. Ever since..." I didn't want to tell her about my eating disorder. It would spark a long worry-filled discussion, and I was all discussion-ed out over the topic.

"Ever since?" She snapped open a pack of brown, crinkly cookies, offering me one. The air filled with the scent of cinnamon, nutmeg, and other goodness. "Gingersnaps. They go perfectly with the cocoa."

"I've never had a gingersnap before."

"Oh, you must try it then."

"No, thanks." If I ate now, I'd only feel the urge to throw it up. Anxiety and food had never mixed well for me, but I was learning to deal with it.

"You sure? It's a camp tradition, started by Ms. Daisy herself." She plucked something else out of the picnic basket—a small flask. She held that up as well. "Among other things."

My eyes snapped open. "Ms. Caroline, is that alcohol?"

"Peppermint schnapps."

I looked at her sideways. "You know I'm fourteen, right?"

"I never said it was for you, silly goose. It's only a little bit. For me." Her face melted into a wry smile. She poured some of the peppermint schnapps into her hot cocoa, took her finger, and stirred the drink a few seconds. Adults could be so weird.

"That was more than a little," I said. She shot me a warning look, then poured more into her cup. "Ms. Caroline!"

She brought the odd concoction up to her mouth, breathing in the vapors. "Julia, when you get to be my age, you allow yourself a few extra liberties. Do you think the FBI is watching?"

I laughed uneasily. "Out here in the middle of nowhere? Sure."

She sipped. "Let's get around to the reason for my visit. Do you know what you're going to say for the dedication? I figured if I put you in this predicament, the least I could do is help."

I shrugged. Of course I didn't know. "'Thank you, everyone, for coming. I wish Elizabeth didn't have

She stared at me a long time. "I would."

I shook my head.

"But if you're not ready, you're not ready, and forcing the issue won't help. Why don't you come have dinner in a while and spend time with the girls? It might help you clear your head." She patted my hand and moved to the door to check on the rain.

I loved Ms. Caroline, but she didn't get it. It didn't work that way. I couldn't just join the girls after all the bonds had already been formed and expect them to treat me the same way they treated their other friends. Even if I'd been here since Day 1, I'd still be the outcast. I was only here because my mom literally made me. Our friendship dynamics had already been set in stone, and little could be done to change that.

Ms. Caroline must've seen the frustration on my face, because she said, "Call your mother, Julia. Let her know you arrived safely. She knows from me, but she'd much prefer to hear your voice. Then we'll see how you're doing later. That sound okay?"

I understood the subtext in what she meant—if I was still in one piece after calling my mom and hanging with the girls, then maybe I could write the speech. But if I was still too upset about being here, she'd be fine with letting me go home.

Fair enough.

"There's one problem," I said.

"What is that?"

"You took my phone." All campers had their digital devices safely put away at the beginning of their stay, in order to encourage face-to-face conversations and lasting, meaning friendships.

"I'll get it for you." Ms. Caroline turned back to the open doorway. The rain was letting up. Big noisy drops fell from the edge of the gutter. "Elizabeth died at such a young age. No mother should ever have to bury her child, not even your aunt, being who she is."

I blinked at the random comment, erupting from the depths of her soul so suddenly. But I appreciated it. Getting past the niceties, the cocoa and gingersnaps, to the heart of what we were both feeling, why we were here together in this little cabin at this exact moment in time.

She looked at me. "But nobody's words, not even her mother's, could do her memory justice. Only yours could. You knew her like nobody did, Julia. Nobody."

THREE

After a dinner of salad with roasted butternut squash, which I ate mostly to keep Ms. Caroline from calling my mom, I wandered out of the mess hall, aimlessly following Cassie and Tori underneath a clear night of bright, twinkling stars.

I didn't know where we were headed, and I didn't care. I only played the part of happy camper. I pretended to care about the conversations that should've sounded normal but felt more alien than anything. Who could talk about ordinary things like boys, school, and social media influencers when a huge, obvious fact silently hung suspended over all our heads?

That Elizabeth had been killed. Killed by a gunman. Because our society was sicker than ever. That was why I was here. Even in 2039, we couldn't do anything to protect her. For the most part, I hated the world I lived in. Except for my family, of course, my dog Ewok, and small pleasures like chatting with my online friend, Yugi.

Here at camp, I never felt more out of place in my life, and Cassie, deciding it was time to address the elephant in the room, finally brought it up. "It must be hard for you to be back after two years," she said, abruptly ending her discussion about the boy Tori was crushing on back home.

I had enjoyed hearing about Aidan, who may or may not like Tori back, considering the mysterious and questionable evidence he'd provided her so far, because at least it was keeping the attention off of me. *Here we go...*

"I guess you could say that," I replied and shoved my hands in my pockets. I felt the smooth paper of Lizzie's envelope. A message from beyond the grave. The more I thought about it, the more I doubted I'd ever be able to open it. Best to place it back where I'd found it.

"We figured you wouldn't come last year," Cassie said. "But when they finished the remembrance garden and said we'd be dedicating it at the end of the season, we thought maybe they'd invite you."

"And here I am," I declared with open arms.

We'd stopped walking. I looked up from the dirt path to see where we were. We'd arrived at said beautiful circular garden filled with all sorts of flowers and plants, an angel statue, another statue of a woman sitting on a bench with a man, young and happy, and in love. Four stone benches facing east, south, west, and north. It was strange to see this where there used to be an empty field for games last time I was here.

"And here we have Ms. Daisy with her husband," Tori explained, showing me the young couple. "It took some getting used to not having the field, but I'm starting to like it."

Ms. Daisy was the woman who'd trained Ms. Caroline, the camp administrator who ran the camp when my mom used to attend. I'd heard nice things

"I don't, Julia, but if you don't want to be there, then let's get you on a plane home tomorrow. I'm sorry I didn't think this through, but you never told me how you felt either. Getting anything out of you has been difficult." Mom's image blinked for a second. She wiped the corner of her eye before focusing back on me.

"I didn't say anything, because you're right—I *am* the best person to honor Lizzie. In theory, I am. I knew her better than anyone, but that doesn't mean I *want* to do this. Or that I'm ready. I thought I was."

"Then we don't need to go through with this, honey. They can find someone else. Please put Ms. Caroline back on the phone. I'll tell her a ride will be there to pick you up in the morning." Mom tapped her fingers onto a keyboard out of view.

"No." I squeezed my eyes shut. "I can do this. I'm just pissed nobody seems to care. I don't think you understand just how much, because well…even I didn't know until I got here."

"That's not fair, Julia. We all care. Very much."

"But no one's considered how hard this if for me to be here."

"Yes, that makes sense. The camp, your surroundings…the memories come back. It's stirred up an emotional response in you. I get it." Mom's eyes filled with distress. She'd always been a good mother who'd tried her best to help me through anything, but I'd never told her how I felt deep down.

In many ways, I blamed her, my dad, my aunt, my grandparents, all the adults of their generation for allowing this to happen. Yes, the rally had been filled with security measures, but why—*why* did those security measures need to be there in the first place? How had we gotten to the point where there was so much hate in our country, so much division? How had we gotten to the point where preparing for a mass shooter was so...*normal*?

"Julia?" Mom blinked. "What are you thinking, honey?"

"You don't want to know. Nobody does. That's what I'm scared of, that my speech isn't going to come out the way everyone thinks it will. I'm upset, Mom. Not just at the person who killed her, but at everyone for not doing enough."

Mom sighed. "I knew there was more going on."

She was alluding to the underlying cause for my eating disorder. My therapist had told her we'd get to the bottom of it eventually. Well, here we were.

"We've been trying. Aunt Emma has done amazing work to change the laws, and—"

"I know," I cut her off, my voice harboring more anger than I was used to showing. Aunt Emma had been instrumental in enacting change, even in the face of harmful old styles of leadership. But the change came too late. It came after we'd already lost Lizzie. What about our parents? And our parents' parents? Had they tried harder to change gun laws, I might not have been in this position. And how did they let so much divisive hatred and anger grow in our country?

"But you still feel we failed you." Mom guessed.

I didn't answer—couldn't.

She sighed heavily, pressing her hands to her eyes. "I'll get you a flight home tomorrow."

"No." I checked over my shoulder to see if anyone was listening, but I was alone. Good, because I didn't need an audience. Not yet. "I can do this. Just give me time. I don't need anyone's help. Tell Ms. Caroline not to visit me in the Writer's Hut anymore. I'll figure this out on my own."

FOUR

I rushed up the creaky steps of Camp Infremo and bolted inside like a whirling dervish on a mission to destroy. Cassie and Tori, getting their toiletries baskets ready to take to the restrooms for bedtime prep, chattered the way they always did. The other girls in our cabin either read or flipped through assorted old-school NatGeo magazines. All paused with deer-in-the-headlights looks when they saw me.

"Julia. We're so sorry," Cassie said, the corners of her blue eyes drooped with helplessness. That was the worst part of accepting people's condolences—they didn't know what to do, or say, or how to act, and their facial expressions always reflected it. It put me in the awkward position of comforting *them*.

"We didn't realize you'd react that way, or we wouldn't have taken you to the memorial. We just thought you might want to see it, that's all." For once, Tori's apology seemed to have come from a real place. I believed her.

But I couldn't bother with either of them, not now. The girls of Camp Auctus may as well have been flickers of the past with their thin attempts to care. My only goal now was to face my own mixed feelings head-on so I wouldn't become a ghost myself.

"Don't worry, I'm fine." I reached up onto my bunk and grabbed my duffel bag, my second pair of shoes from the floor, and my toiletries bucket. If I was going to stay, I had to make it count—by leaving.

"Where are you going?" Cassie asked.

"There's something I need to do," I explained, rolling up my blanket and shoving it into my bag. "I can't here, in this cabin, I mean."

"We said we were sorry, Julia," Tori said. "You don't have to leave."

"It's not you," I assured her, then looked at her more seriously. "It's not."

"Is it for the memorial?" Cassie asked.

"Not really." Yes, I was here to muster up special words for the Summer's End Show, but the fire I felt inside had nothing to do with making others feel better. It had to do with me. "For myself," I said and left.

Like a prisoner breaking out of Alcatraz, I crossed the campus, a bee toward the last flower on earth, my towel slipping off my shoulders. I hustled away. From Cabin Macto, I saw Naomi and Tinay spotting me, who for about two seconds looked like they might challenge me. They must've seen the madwoman look on my face and decided against it.

"Hi, Julia," Tinay only said.

I gave her a curt nod and cut right into the pine needle trail, the one that led deep into the woods with one, lonesome electric lamp to light the path. At the end of the walkway sat the Writer's Hut, dark and alone, a relic of the past, a reminder that written communication was dead. Inside was the laptop, the chair, the couch, the pine needles littered on the floor, all calling out to me.

I entered the cabin and dumped my stuff onto the couch, pulling shut the curtain and flicking on the only desk lamp. The cabin walls lit up with a warm yellow glow. Someone had opened the window, and the curtains billowed from the lake's breezes. From my duffel bag, I plucked out my welcome gift bag containing a green and white Camp Auctus mug, set it on the desk, and filled it with new pens and pencils from a plastic store bag someone had left. I also took out loose sheets of paper and set them next to the computer, placing a pencil on top.

Almost ready.

Something was missing, something that belonged in this room just as much as these ancient writing implements I'd be using to invoke my memories. Two years ago, I had started writing a book in this cabin most of the other girls saw as punishment. But to me, the Writer's Hut was a meditation corner, an isolated house to silence the constant barrage of thoughts long enough to reach the subconscious.

Since I wasn't obligated to join camp activities this time around like two years ago, I would use the seclusion to my highest advantage. I looked around, thinking about how I could make the place more my own. From my duffel bag, I took out the photo of my mom, dad, grandparents, and I on vacation at the Hemingway Home in Key West. Lizzie had loved all the photos of the home's six-toed cats I'd shared with her. Maybe the spirit of the classic author would inspire me.

I remembered what else was missing. I reached into my back pocket—Lizzie's pink envelope. The loopy, cursive handwriting. She'd made it a point in fourth grade to learn the obsolete art, so she could read her grandparents' love letters to each other. I smoothed it against my chest then set it up against the pencil mug.

JULIA...it whispered from bygone days, an invitation to write back, write to her. Everyone wanted to know what it was like being here when it happened, my thoughts, my point of view. If they wanted to know so badly, I would give it to them. They may not like it, though.

You're lucky you weren't with her, many said after the shooting.

Thank God you were at camp when it happened, others declared.

Nobody understood—not a single soul.

I took the broom from the tiny back closet and began to sweep up the littered pine needles. Nobody understood what it was like losing my cousin and best friend, what it was like not being there to protect her. Nobody understood what it was like feeling as though I'd been left behind, a lonely coward who'd refused to take risks, to come along on her trip, who'd chosen to hide away, who'd been stubborn as hell and used guilt against her best friend.

And for what? To prove a point.

JULIA... the letter whispered to me.

I flipped it down so I wouldn't see my name. I left it there as a reminder that Lizzie had been here, once upon a time. Here at Lake Bradford, where she'd left me two summers ago, where an invisible hand had reached down from the sky and protected me from harm. I never deserved getting spared. I should've been there for Lizzie. I should've been there to protect her.

I crammed the backs of my hands against my eyelids.

"Julia?"

I whirled, heart pounding in my ribcage. It was Ms. Caroline at the door which swung lightly in the breeze. The nightly smell of the woods filtered into the room. "Hi." Apparently, Mom had forgotten to ask her not to visit me here for a while.

"Sweetheart, the girls came in as I was getting off the phone with your mother. They said…" She looked frazzled, at a loss to help me or even know where to begin. "Oh, goodness."

"It's okay, Ms. C. I'm not mad at them. They thought I would want to see the new memorial. I was caught by surprise, that's all."

"You're mad at me," she said.

"I'm not."

"Your mother then."

"Not really. Not directly. Ms. Caroline, tonight I realized how much I haven't spoken out loud. There's a lot in here." I gestured to my chest, my ribcage, which felt like it might explode. "I think I've been holding it in."

"I understand. I'm not entirely sure this is a good solution, though," she said, looking around the room. "This cabin is quite a distance from the others. The restrooms are not nearby. What if you need something? What if you…"

"I'll be fine. This is a safe place. I know it is."

"I'd rather you be near us."

Suddenly, I realized what she was afraid of. "I'm not going to..." *Hurt myself,* I almost said, but I wouldn't put the words out there. Doing so would give them energy, and I really needed Ms. Caroline to know I'd be fine. I would never take my own life. I knew she was worried. "I just need space. Maybe coming here was good for me in some ways. But don't worry about the girls. They didn't do anything wrong. I just want to be alone."

Ms. Caroline exhaled, resigned to let me do things my way. It was the least she could do. "Fine. But I am going to leave you with your cell phone. In case you need it."

"I don't need it, Ms. C."

"You sure you'll be fine?"

"As sure as needles point North."

Slowly, a smile appeared, replacing the worry lines on her face. "I suppose now I can say I knew bestselling author Julia Weissman as a young woman. She used to lock herself up away from the other campers in order to write her stories."

"Like a true author."

"Never doubted it for a second. I will respect your process, Julia." She gave me a sad, lingering look, returning five minutes later with a cooler full of water bottles, drinks, halves of sandwiches prepared in the mess hall, sealed containers of fruit, and even a vanilla cupcake. On top was a gingersnap cookie sinking into the frosting.

She winked at me. "For good luck."

Once she was gone, I was alone in the cabin and made sure the door was closed, as best as I could shut it, pulled up my chair close to the desk, and opened up the writing app made to look like a typewriter from last century. It changed the keyboard sounds to a clickety-clack I found rather comforting and even let me change the color paper or style stationery on which I was writing.

I stared at Lizzie's envelope.

There were words inside, words she'd left me with. Too bad I'd never read them. Focusing on the American flag, I allowed my mind to go back to when it all began, the summer of my twelfth year. The year Elizabeth begged me to join her at camp. I didn't think I'd have fun, but I came along anyway. Because if Elizabeth said I'd love it, then it had to be true.

FIVE

2039—

I'd never been on an airplane before. Not because my family hadn't traveled or because my mother hadn't tried to get me on one—trust me, she had—but because I was always terrified. In the movies, good things rarely happened on airplanes. It was always some man sweating at takeoff, or a desperate woman asking the flight attendant for wine, or a crying baby who seemed to know something bad was about to happen.

For some people, hospitals freaked them out. For me, it was plane travel.

And yet, there I was, on a plane to Boston. How did my mom convince me? She didn't.

Elizabeth did.

Elizabeth Richards was my cousin and best friend. Her mother was Senator Emma Singletary-Richards who met my mother at Camp Auctus many summers ago when they were both fourteen and instantly became best friends. According to both my mother and aunt, they hatched a plan like the twin girls in an old movie called *The Parent Trap* to get my grandmother Wendy and granddad Daniel together.

The plan had worked. By the end of the year, Wendy and Daniel had married, and my mom and Emma were sisters. They wouldn't have to be the only child any longer.

That was the story, and if my family was good at anything, it was telling stories. But for now, this was the story of how Elizabeth finally convinced me to leave my safe and sheltered cocoon of a home in Boca Raton and venture out into the world to experience Massachusetts, friendship, paddleboat races, cicadas, and ghost stories around a campfire.

"Look, you can see the airport," Lizzie said, pointing across my chest at Logan Airport way down below. "From there, we rent a car, and from there we drive all the way out west to Camp Auctus. You're going to love it!"

"If you say so," was always my response. Lizzie had spent years telling me how much I would love Camp Auctus, if only I agreed to go, but me being the introvert that I was, always preferred to spend my summers indoors, reading, writing or watching movies. I guess you could say that stories and books were my thing.

Lizzie had always accepted the withdrawn side of me, just like I'd always accepted the extrovert, outdoorsy side of her, and we never got on each other's case about it. We were just different, yet perfect complements to each other. This was her fourth year attending Camp Auctus for Girls and my first.

I had just turned twelve on May 13th. She, on the other hand, would still be eleven for four more weeks. Yes, my mom and her mom had even been pregnant at the same time. They may as well have been twins.

From the seats behind me, my parents talked about the next steps they'd take after the plane landed—where the car rental was, making sure I had everything, stopping at BuyMart for last-minute items. Mom worried, would I be okay? Would I make friends? Would I fit in? My father told her everything would be fine, and if anyone would have a hard time adjusting, it was Mom while I was gone.

"You know I can hear you guys, right?" I told my parents.

One of Mom's green eyes peered at me between the seats. "Sorry." Her eyebrow arched, as her voice amplified amidst the thrum of the engine by the narrowed space.

"My mom was the same way the first time I came," Lizzie explained, folding up her tray table and putting her personal devices away. She rolled her eyes. "She'll be fine."

Lizzie was traveling with us, because her parents were doing important work on the campaign trail. U.S. Senator Emma Singletary-Richards from Florida (my aunt) had a lot of people to meet and things to talk about if she was going to have a successful race. She'd declared her intention to run for president back in February and was now putting together committees of people to help Americans solve a bunch of different problems.

Like I said, important work. But in a way, I felt sorry for Lizzie. She didn't get to see her mom that much. Aunt Emma was always working in another state, even though they 'grammed every day. But still.

That was why Lizzie was at my house half the time, why Grandma Wendy and Granddad had been her caretakers for most of the summer.

"I'm so exciteeeeddddd." Lizzie gripped my arm so hard, I thought it would fall off. "When we get there, I'm going to introduce you to everybody— Cassie, Tori, Naomi, Uleili, Hannah, Tinay…well Tinay can be kind of salty, but she's really nice when you get to know her."

"In other words, she's mean," I said. When Lizzie thought of someone as "really nice when you get to know her," it meant the girl was difficult, and either Lizzie couldn't see it or she just gave everybody the benefit of the doubt. But that was what made her special—the way she got along with everybody.

"No, they're all great. You'll see. Ah!" She could barely contain her excitement. "I'm so happy you finally get to meet all the girls I've been telling you about for so long."

"Yay," I faked enthusiasm. "I hate people. I hate the world." I laughed. I liked people just fine. I just hated being in new situations. "Whatever you say, Lizzie."

Apparently, you had to tie a green ribbon in your hair when you first arrived at Camp Auctus. It was some tradition that'd been around for like a hundred years. It symbolized "getting things done." You know, putting your hair up and all that, instead of relaxing and unwinding. Unlike vacation, Camp Auctus was big on making you do things, getting you up out of your seat, making you vocal, making you think, basically engaging young women. It was big on traditions, on connecting with the natural world and ancient ways of doing stuff, and I had no clue how I was going to survive without my shows for a *whole* summer. When you left Camp Auctus, tradition was you took off your green ribbon and tossed it out the window. The camp administrators, Ms. Caroline and Ms. Susan, spent a day picking them all up off the ground.

"Grandma Wendy did it, my mom did it, I've done it," Lizzie bragged.

"I guess that means my mom's tossed the green ribbon, too."

"I have," Mom added from the front seat.

When we arrived, it looked like a perfectly nice camp. I was nervous when we took all our stuff out of the trunk and parked ourselves into the queuing area by the long tables, but I took the time to glance around at how beautiful the facilities were. In the past, I'd always felt sorry for Lizzie that she couldn't just relax at home, that she had to spend her summers at camp, like it was a death sentence. Hearing about her being sent away every year so her mother could work made me melancholy. But it was actually really beautiful.

Like the perfect June day—hot and muggy, with clear skies and few clouds. There was something intangible in the air when we arrived that I hadn't felt in a long time, not even on the first day of middle school. Excitement, hope, anxiety? Looking around as my parents checked us in, I saw my same emotions on the faces of the younger girls, the ones who seemed to be new to Camp Auctus. Most of the girls my age seemed more at ease with each other. Probably due to the fact that they were used to this routine. They'd all known each other since elementary school.

43

"Cassie!" Lizzie cried out and ran into the arms of a tall girl with blond hair that swung perfectly in long waves from her green ribbon. "I want you to meet my cousin, Julia. Julia, come!"

For the first hour, Lizzie had to tell me "Julia, come!" quite a few times. Apparently, I was doing the introvert thing and hiding alongside my mom, who kept nudging me to go and meet new people. Why didn't non-introverts ever understand that only made things worse? Elbowing me in the ribs to get out from under her wing only made me want to resist.

I groaned. I could do this.

I joined Lizzie and waved at this Cassie girl, also at the other girl who came running up to us three and put her arms around Cassie and Lizzie's shoulders. "Yes! You're here! Are we in the same cabin again this year? Oh, my God, I hope so, because I'm so scared of being in Cabin Macto. And oh, my God, who's this?"

"This is Julia, my cousin from Florida. This is her first time."

She may as well have put a shiny new sticker on my forehead, because that was how I felt, like a brand new package to be unboxed and examined by all the girls. Luckily, Cassie and Tori seemed like perfectly normal humans, but I still had to make an effort to smile and relax around them while they and Lizzie did all the talking and I did all the following like a shadow or a homesick puppy.

Every so often, I'd catch my parents' grins from the queue like I was so cute, making new friends already. *Ugh.*

When it turned out that we were all in the same cabin, I immediately let a huge sigh of relief escape me.

Campers were allowed to request who they stayed with, but sometimes the staff made the executive decision to separate the girls so they wouldn't form cliques. Fortunately for me, because I was new and came to camp referred by another camper, they kept us together.

Our cabin—Cabin Infremo.

"My old cabin!" my mom cried. I'd never seen her so giddy, hopping up and down with glee, holding my dad's arm, like if somebody just told her that all 3-wick candles were now free down at the bath and lotion shop.

We signed in and sat in the amphitheater and listened to a fun, quirky lady named Mrs. Caroline who turned out to be the Camp Administrator. Nobody actually introduced her. Nobody had to—everyone knew Mrs. Caroline and cheered for her like a rock star from the moment she came onstage, waving her clipboard around and pumping her fists in triumph.

"You're going to love Ms. C," Lizzie whispered, leaning into me.

The Big Welcome began, and I had to admit I was feeling Pretty Nervous, if overwhelmed, by the things we'd be doing this summer. Important speakers, all of them women, were coming out to meet us each week, from congresswomen to journalists, to celebrities like record producer Deserae McGavin, who Mom said she knew from her Camp Auctus days.

After we got the lowdown on rules and what to expect, we walked around free-greeting other parents and their daughters. Many of the parents were Camp Auctus alumni themselves. My parents shook hands with everyone Lizzie knew, because like her mother, my aunt, the Senator, Lizzie seemed to know the whole world.

Saying goodbye to my parents once we were all settled into our cabins went harder for my mother than it did for me. My dad took pleasure in taking candid shots of Mom dabbing her eyelids while I stood by laughing at her. Yes, I know it's not nice to laugh at your mom when she's crying, but it really was funny.

"Mom, it's only eight weeks," I said, hugging her around the middle.

"And I'm going to take good care of her, Aunt Becca, don't you worry." Lizzie joined in the hug and we giggled in between while my mother's yoga-muscled arms crunched us together.

"I have no doubt about that whatsoever, Elizabeth." Mom wiped her eyes. When she could no longer hold onto our babyhood, Mom turned to each of us and kissed us on the forehead. "Be good, girls. Better yet, be brilliant, my bright young stars."

What a Mom thing to say.

I was about to giggle again when I caught my father giving me a warning look like I better take my mom seriously. This was hard enough for her as it was without me mocking her. I swallowed my laughter and hugged her. "Thanks, Mom. I'll write you letters using mail service. They're going to show us how to do that, right, Liz?"

"Yes, during the first week. How to use stamps, how to properly address an envelope, how to write in cursive...all that old stuff."

"Nice. So I can decode all your mushy letters to each other when I get home. Mwahahaha..." I loved old letters—so romantic—but never had the time to learn

cursive script writing in elementary school like I
wanted to and never got around to researching it myself
like I did so many other lost Old World arts.

"That's so wonderful that they still do that,"
Mom said, finally pulling away. "Anyway, love you
both." She blew her last kisses. I waved them off.
Suddenly, it felt real—they were leaving me two
thousand miles from home.

I hate to say this, but when my mother left, I felt
a flood of relief. As an introvert and an empath, I'd
always picked up others' emotions, and my mom's
anxiety had been suffocating me since we'd landed. I'd
taken all my clues from my father, so when even he got
teary-eyed at the goodbye, I understood the big deal.
Now, alone with the fresh Massachusetts air by
gorgeous Lake Bradford, I could finally get down to
business—finding out what all the fuss was about.
Camp Auctus, I'm finally here to meet you. Sweet
oranges, you would've thought this place was magical
or something. Little did I know, at that moment, how
true that would turn out to be.

SIX

By 11 AM, we'd done archery, by 1 PM, canoeing, and by late afternoon, ceramics.

Camp Auctus didn't play around. They wanted everyone awake by eight, fed and briefed on daily activities by 9 AM, and off to their first activity by 10 AM. Though it was only Tuesday and our first official day, not counting registration yesterday, I was already looking forward to Saturday when we got to sleep in until eleven.

"Every major muscle group hurts," I informed Lizzie over lunch.

"You'll get used to it," she laughed.

At the mess hall, I was happy to see them serving wonderful balanced meals of quinoa, avocado toast, and a variety of hummus dishes. On the car ride over yesterday, Mom had told me how, when she used to attend in 2014, they'd only just begun switching over to healthier meals from macaroni and cheese and hot dogs, and how that was the sort of progressive thing Camp Auctus was known for doing.

"When do we get to relax?" I asked.

"You saw the schedule. Every day, we have sunset meditation by the lake."

"That sounds nice."

"It is. A great way to end part of our day and switch to quieter stuff like singing around the campfire, reading, or—you'll like this part—telling stories."

"Ooo, yes." Now that was what I expected from a campfire. Scary stories were my favorite because it was always interesting to see what different people found frightening. We did them every year at Manatee River Elementary School. When I started middle school, however, seems all fun got wiped off the curriculum.

"After campfire, we have some free time before bed. There's something I want to show you. You're going to love it."

The great thing about being here with Liz was that she knew me so well, she knew ahead of time what I would and wouldn't love. Had I come by myself, none of the existing veteran campers would've known what to show me. I'd have to discover stuff by myself, which I was unlikely to do, seeing that I was only adventurous in my imagination. It was more fun this way, having a partner in crime.

In the evening, we lounged around the campfire, and for the first time ever, I witnessed magic. Real, natural magic. Between the floating, glowing embers of crackling fire logs, the flitting fireflies, and the multitude of stars above, Camp Auctus shone like diamonds against a velvety black forest backdrop. There we were, in the middle of it all, gathered around small bonfires, talking, laughing, whispering.

We didn't sing that first night, but other groups, like Camp Macto, did and two of their girls, Tinay and Naomi, kept leaving the group to come to ours to see what we were doing. There was no rule that said you had to stay with your group for any of the activities. You just had to sleep with them at night. Well, Tinay and Naomi must've been bored and didn't want to sing. As they headed over, Lizzie filled me in.

"We were cabin mates last year. Cabin Inspíra," Lizzie explained. "We had a good year, it's not that we didn't, but we had to work at it. It wasn't a natural fit like our cabin this year. Don't you get the feeling like we all just mesh?"

"I guess so," I answered. "Although I never get the sense that I ever fit anywhere, Lizzie, you know that. You and your mom are just as comfortable in a church choir as you are on a softball team, as you are on a debate team. Me, I'm like a pterodactyl on a beach."

"It's not true," Lizzie laughed, spearing a marshmallow and sticking the end into the flames. "People like you. You just have to give them a chance."

Maybe that was my problem, why I didn't have friends at home, why my cousin constituted pretty much my whole entourage, and why I was okay with that. I would've much preferred hours rubbing Ewok's shaggy brown belly than I was getting to know new people. I was better off with one amazing friend than a gaggle of mediocre ones.

I generally felt like most people weren't sincere. Like they showed you one side of their personality but really hid another. They acted pleasant but could be cruel and callous on the inside. Of course, that could be because I'd had a bad experience with girls like Veronica and Shai in sixth grade, and Tinay and Naomi from Camp Macto reminded me of them. Queen bees looking for a kingdom to rule.

That's what I loved about animals—they showed you the real them. No sneakery.

"I give people chances. They just don't get me. Not everyone wants to gossip, talk about influencers, or be sociable all the time. Some people want to chill. Alone. With dogs." I shoved a toasted marshmallow in my mouth. Mom with her healthy choices made eating six to seven marshmallows in a single sitting impossible.

Lizzie shook her head. "Julia, you're so goth."

I imagined myself dressed all in black, despairing in my angsty teen thoughts. "I'm destined to be alone." We chuckled, but the words still lingered in the air, even as we speared more marshmallows and changed the subject. Sometimes I worried that I loved being alone so much, I'd end up that way for the rest of my life.

"You're crazy. That's why I love you," Lizzie said.

"Thanks for dragging me out here," I replied.

Lizzie looked at me with her bright blue eyes then lay her head on my shoulder. "I'm so glad you came. Now camp feels complete."

I didn't argue. As beautiful as this evening was, as much as I was loving Camp Auctus so far, I'd only done it for her. There wasn't anything about me that Lizzie needed, however, so I was happy just to make her laugh and feel complete.

"Julia, Lizzie says you like writing," someone said. I turned to see Tori making conversation with me. I felt like a huge spotlight had been shined on me.

"Uh... Yeah, I do. I don't know. It's weird. I love writing stories and reading. I know that sounds lame, but I do." It was more than I wanted to say, which was nothing.

"That doesn't sound lame," Tori said. All the other girls around the campfire—Cassie, Tori, Hannah, Ari, and Imogene all agreed. Suddenly, I had an audience.

"That's not lame at all, Julia," Lizzie scoffed. "In fact, I'm jealous of the stuff she comes up with. This one story she wrote last year…"

Lizzie, do not…

"I swear it was just like something JK Rowling would write, or Edwina Graves," she went on.

I whispered, "You can stop now."

"What? It's true. She's really talented. Julia, tell them what your stories are about." And just like that, Lizzie was doing the same thing my mom did whenever she felt proud, trying to sell me to the rest of her friends when all I wanted was to hide under a rock.

"Actually?" I fake yawned. "It's getting kind of late. I'm tired. I'll talk about it tomorrow." I got up, sensing that strangling sensation come over me whenever somebody put me in the spotlight. "Be back in a bit, if that's okay?" I asked our counselor-in-training, Mattie.

"We're wrapping up here in ten minutes, so come right back," Mattie instructed.

"Got it," I said. It was almost Chat Time, a half hour period before getting ready for bed that involved using up all the rest of your energy by talking about whatever topic you wanted. I went for a walk and within seconds, Lizzie rushed by my side. "I am so sorry. I know you hate that. I wasn't thinking."

"It's okay." I headed around the lake on a trail shrouded in darkness.

"No, it's not. I shouldn't have done that. But if it's any consolation, I only said that because I really do love your writing. I wasn't just saying that. I'm actually a big fan."

"My writing's not that great, Lizzie."

"Are you kidding me? Julia, you don't even know how good you are."

"There's a million people better than me."

"That's not the point. The point is you're the only one who writes like you. I can't do what you do."

"No, but you can talk, you can meet people, you get along with everybody, and that is a more special talent than writing."

"Agree to disagree. I have my talents, you have yours. And...I actually have a very good reason why I said all that back there." She huffed and puffed to keep up with me. I didn't know where I was headed, but I had to walk off the discomfort until it dripped out of my head.

"To embarrass me to death?"

"No," she laughed. "To set you up. I was going to tell the girls we should all show you something, but you're getting warm anyway."

"Warm? I mean, yeah, it's hot out."

"You're getting closer....closer..."

"What are you talking about?"

"A little closer...now....stop." She put her hands on my shoulders.

I stopped.

A warm wind blew over the lake and wrapped me up like a chenille blanket. All around were the sounds of cicadas, frogs, and other critters of a Massachusetts summer singing together like a symphony. Then, I saw it—a trail of pine needles leading into the darkness, ending at a little house sitting under one, lone dim lamp. If I didn't know better, I'd have thought it was Hansel & Gretel's house from that old fairy tale.

"What is that?" I asked. "The Witch of the Wood's house?"

"Come on." She tugged my arm and led me down the path to the door of the little wooden structure. Nothing decorated the cabin, no flowers, no wreaths on the outside. Nothing but a sign etched above the door: *Not all who wander are lost.* It was a quote from one of my father's favorite writers of all time, J.R.R. Tolkein, author of *The Lord of the Rings.*

"Is this the Writer's Hut?" I guessed. I knew it was. Lizzie had mentioned it before in one of her end-of-summer rants. Down to the chimney on top.

Biting her lip, she led me inside. She tugged on the light cord, as yellow light filled the room. I fell in love. A cozy couch, a broad desk with a single solitary lamp on it, the lantern we'd turned on hanging from the center of the ceiling, a framed painting of the American flag, a wood-burning stove (to go with the chimney), a round colorful rug, and in the middle of the desk, glowing in its glory, surrounded by golden, glittery light of my overactive imagination…an old typewriter.

"Is that…?"

"It's a computer," Lizzie said. "But it looks vintage, doesn't it?" She waved her hand over its field of energy.

"Hello, Elizabeth. Welcome back." The computer's screen lit up. I had never seen anything like it—so cool.

"Hello, typewriter. We don't need you right now...byeeeee." She shut it down so it wouldn't talk again.

I chuckled. "Does it know me, too?"

"You have to sit and write something for it to remember you." She plopped herself on the couch and crossed her ankles up in the air. "I'll let you and this cabin get acquainted," she said.

"Hello, Writer's Hut. Pleased to make your acquaintance." I could spend hours in here. I could write the next great American novel. For a year now, I'd been waiting for inspiration to strike, so I could become the youngest ever author to write a bestseller.

Her voice filtered through my dream fog. "Am I forgiven now?"

"Yes. Super forgiven."

She chuckled. "And that, ladies and gentlemen..." Lizzie's voice changed to a more modulated adult TV announcer kind, "was the last anyone ever saw of Julia Weissman."

SEVEN

Ms. Susan rang the camp bell, signaling time to come back and get ready for bed, but I couldn't get up from the desk chair. "This is so amazing. Does no one ever come here?"

"No one cares like you do. We have to go, though. Come on." Lizzie pulled on the chair's backrest, tilting me backwards, giggling as I lost my balance.

"Hey!" I gripped the edge of the desk hard.

Suddenly, the door opened. A draft blew in, followed by Ms. Caroline, looking surprised to see us there. "Ah. I saw the lights on and wondered who was here. What are you ladies doing so far from the common area?"

"I was just showing Julia the Writer's Hut. I think she's in love, Ms. Caroline." Lizzie laughed, making her way to the door.

Ms. Caroline strolled in, lovingly touching the walls, chair, and desk. "Well, who could blame her? This is one of my favorite spots on this whole campus, as well. Do you like writing, Miss Weissman?" She paused next to me.

I was about to reply when Lizzie cut me off, "She likes isolation."

"Um…" I gave her a dirty look.

"I'm kidding. She does write. She's going to be an author when she grows up. Her books are going to sell gajillions of copies."

"Lizzie…" I covered my eyes. She didn't have to make such a fuss about it. She didn't have to answer for me either. I told Ms. Caroline, "I write stories, but I never finish anything."

"What's the most you've written?" Ms. Caroline asked.

"I wrote four chapters of a book once. Came out to about twenty pages." I remembered a story I wrote during 4th grade when my teacher, Mrs. Helane, got diagnosed with cancer, so for the rest of the school year, there wasn't much for us to do because of how distracted she was.

"That's a lot for someone your age. I can't write that much. I get distracted or sit around too long waiting for the muse to visit, which never does. Consider yourself a serious writer. Color me impressed." Ms. Caroline sounded funny, using language I'd only heard from Grandma Wendy or Granddad.

I didn't know what the muse was, but I felt uncomfortable being the center of attention again. I stood from the desk and moved to the door near the safety of Lizzie's presence. I'd have to come back to this cabin as soon as possible. It was the perfect little getaway.

Ms. Caroline had more things to say. I was starting to understand that she was a really personable woman. "Are your parents writers, too?"

I shook my head. "My dad, not really. My mom likes poetry and writing songs."

"Ah, yes. I remember. Your mother passed that on to you. She loved to write. It always amazes me how we're the continuation of our parents' lives, as much as we like to think of ourselves as individuals. Right, Elizabeth?"

She smiled at Lizzie secretively, as though hoping that Lizzie would go into politics like her mother and grandmother, our Grandma Wendy, who used to be a Senator from Texas a long time ago. I understood why. Lizzie was so sociable, so extrovert, shaking hands with people, trying to help others all the time. One day she'd change the world. She was so good at making an impression, it made me envious.

"Anyway, skedaddle." Ms. Caroline waved us away. "Time for bed. We'll talk more tomorrow, and my goodness, does this place need a good cleaning." The woman pulled a broom from behind the door and began sweeping pine needles outside.

We started down the path, and Lizzie turned around to walk backwards. "Can Julia use the Writer's Hut whenever she wants?" she asked.

"During Free Time, of course," Ms. Caroline replied. Of course. I wouldn't expect to be allowed to live in the Writer's Hut all day long, avoiding camp activities.

Although that would be a dream come true.

A huge dream.

The next day, we spent the morning canoeing across Lake Bradford. Because it was early enough, the air was cool, the water even cooler, and there was a briskness about the lake that felt so different from Florida. A morning at home during summer would've felt like a hot oven being left open for all the heat to spill out. But this was the perfect temperature. I would definitely come back to Massachusetts again next year if Lizzie still wanted me along. If only I could make friends like she could.

For canoeing, I got paired with Uleili from Cabin Inspíra. We had to work together in order to get the canoe to move straight. Two oar strokes on the left, two oar strokes on the right. Rinse. Repeat. Sitting in the back, I had the power to steer the boat and make it go left or right, while Uleili just followed whatever I did.

I liked this activity. I didn't have to speak too much or make uncomfortable conversation. Our actions complemented each other, but there was still communication involved. Uleili and I managed to reach the other side of the lake and back without bumping into any other canoes more than twice, but I was a little jealous that Lizzie and Cassie rowed perfectly, bumped into nothing, and led the pack like pros.

By the time we returned to camp, we were so utterly exhausted, our CITs gave us two hours of free time, and while everyone else collapsed in the cabins for post-rowing naps, I showered, changed into fresh shorts and T-shirt, and escaped to the Writer's Hut. I wasn't sure if we needed to tell anyone we were going, or if we were allowed to go alone, but I couldn't imagine going to the Writer's Hut with someone else to distract you. Maybe this was why the hut wasn't so popular with the campers.

For me, it was heaven. Lizzie was right. I loved isolation.

When I pulled open the door to the cabin, however, someone was sitting in there.

"Oh. I'm sorry." I began closing the door.

"No, it's okay." A girl stood from the chair, put away paper and pencil, and turned. She wore glasses and had curly brown hair with rainbow colors on the tips. "You can have it. I couldn't write anything."

"Couldn't think of anything?"

"It's harder than I thought. I have a million ideas, but when it comes time to write them, I can't write anything good. You can have it," she said again, brushing by me with a smile and leaving the room.

I watched her leave. It had gotten cloudy the last few minutes, and the fragrant scent of rain was in the air. Being from Florida, I was a rain expert. I could tell this was a huge one—a solid hour-long deluge headed this way, the kind that shut everything down. There were few things I loved more than thunderstorms to put me in the writing mood.

The cabin window was open. I thought about closing it before realizing it'd be hot inside if I did, but rain meant a breeze, so I left it open. The flimsy curtains blew softly. I pulled the chair out and sat at the desk, running my hands over the smooth wood, loving the feel.

"Hello, Julia." The computer's screen lit up, the part supposed to look like a sheet of paper in the vintage typewriter. It even typed out H-E-L-L-O, J-U-L-I-A in old-style letters with the clickety-clack sound.

"Hello."

"What would you like to write? A letter? A poem, perhaps?"

"None of the above. Silent, please." I giggled.

"As you wish. Enjoy your afternoon."

"Thanks." I took a deep breath and let it out slow.

What did I want to write about? Well, this whole experience of being here with Lizzie, for one. Even though we spent time together at home, here, we were in a whole new world. A world where she was friends with other girls, and I was an outsider, even after two days. Could I be friends with her without being jealous?

I wanted Lizzie to be who she was, but I was also terrified of her hanging out with other girls, leaving me out of stuff. It was a fear I had to get over. Maybe I would write about our summer together in an effort to sort my feelings out. I could call it *Summer Lost & Reborn*. I wasn't sure why. I just liked the title. I tapped on the keyboard.

I...*click.*

T...*clack.*

Closing my eyes, I thought about the day we arrived, how nervous I felt, how my mother was more excited than I was because she'd come to this camp too as a girl. And then, I just started to type:

It was the summer of 2039.

I looked outside. *A beautiful summer day.*

And then, the words just came, like they did anytime I isolated myself. I wrote for a long time. I wasn't sure how long, because I didn't bother to find the clock function on the computer. It was hidden, which was perfect. No distractions. I wrote about my first day, but I changed the name of the character to Julian instead of Julia. Super stretch of the imagination, I know.

The best part about it was: nobody came for me. Here I was, all alone in this cabin, tapping away at the typewriter, telling a story, allowing my mind to unleash whatever it wanted. I didn't worry about how professional it sounded, if there were mistakes, or anything trivial. I just wrote. I imagined myself as one of my favorite authors from long ago, isolated and pouring out their hearts with stories of kings and queens, aliens and monsters, romance and unicorns.

I imagined myself as an author in the future, selling millions of books, signing copies at bookstores. Not many bookstores left in the world, but I loved them. The smell of old paper, the leather of cozy chairs, the rows and rows of books, each one containing an entire universe. Would people ever read my words? Probably not. But a girl could dream, right? And I guess that was the best part of Camp Auctus—the openness to dream.

Two hours must've gone by before someone finally knocked at the door. I heard them talking before they reached the hut. The sounds of girls, not Ms. Caroline, chattered outside.

"Come in," I said, just as I was finishing a sentence. It wasn't my last one, but it would be a good place to stop.

Lizzie appeared with Tori and Cassie in tow. "Thought we might find you here."

"I have a feeling you're going to be saying that a lot."

Her gaze tried to get past me, onto the screen. "Did you get to write anything?"

"Yes, a lot. This cabin is the best place in the world."

Lizzie exchanged looks with Cassie. "What did I tell you? Soon we'll rename the hut 'Birthplace of the American Author Jules Weissman,'" she added dramatically with a wave of her hand.

"And they'll rename Cabin Infremo 'the Birthplace of Famous American Quantum Physicist Cassie Lorigo,'" Cassie said with an air swipe of her own hand.

Lizzie giggled. "Guess there's a lot of future famous women here. I can't wait for all of us to actually become influential people. But there's a whole world out there, princess, and you're missing it. We're going to take a walk down to the stable to check on Apple, now that it's stopped raining. Then meditation by the lake. Are you coming?"

. "Yes," I mumbled and faced the computer, "Shutting down."

Now that I'd gotten nine pages of words down on paper, I could hang with the girls, and finally rejoin the outside world.

EIGHT

I visited the Writer's Hut every day that week, especially since Ms. Caroline seemed to encourage it. Every time I'd walk past her, she'd say, "There goes the famous novelist!" It always made me feel special.

I'd write during Free Time, of course, but if I could've snuck out after bedtime to get an extra word count down, I would've done that, too. As it was, whenever Ms. Susan rang the bell for us to reconvene as a group, I felt annoyed I wasn't able to finish the thought I was on.

The girls had started a drama group in one of the amphitheater's backstage rooms, and Lizzie had asked me a couple times to give up the writing time in order to participate.

"I want to," I'd said, "but I already started the book. I'm getting to a good part now. You know my goal is to finish it before summer's over. It'd be so cool to come home and show everybody what I accomplished. Wouldn't it?"

"Yes! That'd be so great. *But* we could use one more person for the skit," Lizzie insisted. "And I really want that person to be you, Julia. We haven't spent much time together since you started writing the book."

She pouted.

I groaned. I didn't want to be a stick in the mud (as Grandma Wendy always said). I had to participate in some things. I had joined camp, after all, to be with my cousin. I sighed. "What's the skit about?"

Her eyes lit up with happiness. "It's based on *Little Women.* I'm Jo, Cassie is Meg, Tori is Beth, and we need an Amy, but we're making up our own scene. In our skit, the sisters are getting ready for a Halloween party."

"There was no Halloween in the time of *Little Women*," I said.

"I know, that's why we're *making up* our own scene." Lizzie laughed. "It's just a free play exercise."

"I don't want to be Amy. I wouldn't make a good Amy." Inside my stomach, alarm bells were going off at the thought of performing. I could already see the judging eyes of the audience and my cheeks flushing with embarrassment.

"You'd make a perfect Amy! Come on, Julia, please. Maybe the skit will inspire new scenes for your book." She tugged on my arm, leading me to the amphitheater where the girls were already practicing.

"I'm already inspired. I don't need to act to feel inspired."

Still, I went. I wanted to make Lizzie happy. It was true that sometimes you had to step away from your story in order to let ideas grow and blossom. But acting in a skit? My worst nightmare. Next thing you knew, we'd be onstage, performing in front of the whole camp. Then, in front of a whole amphitheater of parents.

Ugh. No way.

"Can't I make the costumes instead?" I asked once we were all together. I opened a closet full of outfits, feather boas, hats, and sequined dresses, pulling them out, one by one, creating a colorful heap on the wood floor. "I feel like I'd make a better costume designer than an Amy." I could hear the shakiness in my own voice.

The other girls just shrugged, deferring to Lizzie who apparently was doubling as an actress *and* director. She gave me a mournful look. "I was really looking forward to you playing Amy."

"It would be a good compromise," I said with a shrug.

"I think that would work fine," Cassie said, tossing her mane of light brown hair into a bun and tying it. "This scene is about Jo, Beth, and Meg anyway. Amy was just going to be sitting off to the side, watching them try on different costumes. We were going to have her say, 'Can I please wear the bear costume? Oh, please, Meg, I promise to be a good bear!'"

I cringed. "That's not a good line. Cutting it would help the play."

Cassie and Tori laughed. They understood I meant it as a joke to serve my own desire not to speak, but for a fraction of a second, I saw it—Lizzie's look of disappointment in me.

"Besides," I added, "you need people behind the scenes as much as in front of the scenes for a good play to work."

Her gaze held mine for what felt like a terribly long five seconds. "Fine, whatever. Do the costumes, Julia. I don't care." She turned her back on me.

Cassie and Tori gaped at each other without a word.

Ouch.

The last time I'd heard Lizzie be that cold to me was in second grade when we were coloring the same printed banner for Aunt Emma's birthday. Lizzie had colored the bricks gray at one end while I colored them red at the other, and when we discovered we were coloring the brick wall different colors, she got mad, threw the crayon, and left me with a bi-colored drawing of Humpty Dumpty.

"Fine, I'll be Amy." I sighed, throwing down a pink feather boa. Everyone turned to me. "As long as I don't have to speak, I can sit on the floor like I'm watching Jo and Meg and laugh at their antics, and that'll be enough. The scene isn't about Amy anyway."

"Great, let's do it. We're running out of time," Lizzie said without another thought. I was bothered that she couldn't detect the hurt in my voice at her making me do something I didn't want to do.

"But it's not until next week," Cassie said.

"Wait, what's not until next week?" I asked, panic rising in my throat.

Lizzie stared at Cassie. "Why did you say that?"

"I thought she knew," Cassie said, shrugging. "Look, it's no big deal, Julia. We're just performing it in front of Cabin Inspíra."

"Is that it?" I asked. "Not in front of the whole camp or anything?"

"Maybe ten other people. It'll be fine. I promise." Lizzie held onto my elbow. "So let's do this already."

"You know, you're doing it all wrong,"

someone outside of our little circle spoke.

We turned to find Tinay standing at the door, studying us while holding onto the door frame. "*Julia* looks like a Meg, *Lizzie* looks like a Beth, and *Cassie* looks like a Jo. If anyone should be sitting on the floor like an Amy, it's Tori." She smiled brightly. "Sorry, I just came in to use the bathroom and heard you all arguing."

"We weren't arguing," Lizzie said, peeved by the unsolicited opinion.

Tinay tapped the door frame. "I'm only in the Drama Club at my school for the fourth year in a row, but what do I know?" She walked off toward the bathrooms.

"Who cares if she's in Drama Club?" Cassie whispered.

"Yeah, go back to your Songs of *Hamilton* Poetry Slam Group. As if she knows anything about *Hamilton*," Tori mumbled. "If anyone knows *Hamilton*, it's me. My mom raised me on the soundtrack. She'd make me sing with her every night while making dinner," Tori mumbled. She began reciting the first lyrics of the musical out loud.

"You know what? She's right." Lizzie said, looking up suddenly. "The casting is all wrong. Julia is *so* a Meg."

What? No. I stared at her. I would not be a Meg. Not, not, no, no.

Tinay was back, hand on hip, laser-focused on Tori, ears perked and listening. "Did you say you know *Hamilton*?"

Tori scoffed then crossed her arms. "First of all, who doesn't know *Hamilton*? It's only the most important work of musical art of the 21st Century. And second, I guarantee I know *Hamilton* better than anyone in your group—I'm saying that in the friendliest way possible, Tinay, without being a total diva about it— and I'm willing to put my money where my mouth is."

"Great." Tinay smiled, impressed with Tori's declaration of independence. "Come to our group, then. If your mama raised you on *Hamilton*, then we could use you. Come on."

"Sorry, guys." Tori got up, brushed off her shorts. "I have to be in the *Hamilton* group. I have trained all my life for this. My mom would disown me if she knew I'd passed, and *I am not giving away my...shot.* Ha! Get it?" And then, in a poof of Tori-shaped smoke, she was gone.

That left Lizzie, Cassie, and me.

"You know what? It'll be fine," Lizzie said, scratching out a few lines from the script. "Erase, erase, erase. Yup, this is not an issue. This is going to be great." She dotted someone on the script with harsh emphasis.

"Really? We just lost half our Free Time arguing about who will play who, and now we lost Tori, and Julia doesn't want to play any part with a beating heart." Cassie threw her hands up in the air.

"Hey, that's not nice," I said.

"And it's not true either," Lizzie defended me. "Cassie, come on. We don't need Tori."

Cassie wouldn't look at me. I knew she thought that losing her best friend to the Songs of *Hamilton* Poetry Slam Group was somehow my fault for being wishy-washy about who I wanted to play. If we hadn't been arguing about it, Tinay wouldn't have overheard.

And if Tinay hadn't overheard, she never would've stolen Tori away from our group.

"Besides, *Hamilton* is about the founding fathers," I said, trying to smooth things over. "And we should be focused on *her*stories not *his*tories," I added proudly. Why were they even performing *Hamilton* when this a camp about female empowerment?

"Julia…" Lizzie hugged her clipboard. "Will you play Meg?"

My cheeks blew up with air. "Do I have to speak?"

"YES!" Both she and Cassie half-yelled at me. *My GOD, okay…*

"Fine." My stomach crunched just thinking about it, but I had to force myself into these new situations. I had to or never hear the end of it. Cassie and Lizzie got into places onstage and went over the first lines while I bit my lip and cringed. "But only one line, okay?"

Lizzie and Cassie both glared at me.

NINE

CIT Patty lined us up for sprint running. Fifty-yard dashes up and down the track, in different groups of ten, for about an hour. The point, I guess, was to see who could run the fastest and had the most stamina, because before we knew it, all the 11 and 12-year-olds were being told to split into groups of four, regardless of cabin assignment.

"Relay races," Lizzie said, bending at the waist to catch her breath. "Now we have to see who goes first, second, third…anchor."

"What's anchor?" I wiped my brow with the hem of my shirt.

"Last person to carry the baton—the one who crosses the finish line."

"Oh."

I didn't care who crossed the finish line. It was a scorching day, about 95 degrees with no clouds, so it felt like the sun was trying to rearrange our faces into Picasso paintings. All I cared about was my next cold water bottle. Today would've been a good day for a swim, or an ice cube throwing contest, or Frozen Lemonade Slip 'n' Slide. I'd have to have a talk with Ms. Caroline about this whole relay race nonsense.

Lizzie's cheeks flushed pink. Our group

gathered around Uleili, another kid named Frances, Lizzie, and me. "So it's up to us to decide the order of our team," Lizzie explained, taking the lead, as Lizzie tended to do. "Why don't we do one more quick sprint? Slow and steady should go first, middle two are average runners, and fastest sprinter goes last. We're up against that team." She pointed to the other side of the cones, where two tall girls stood like Amazons, hands on their hips, checking us out, same as we were checking on them.

"We're gonna die," I mumbled.

Lizzie said, "Nah, we can beat them."

"I just want a break," I said.

More than that, I wanted to write the next chapter of my book. All day I'd been visualizing my next scene. What I would give to be inside the Writer's Hut at this moment. I hadn't been in two days, because Free Time was always being used up by something Ms. Caroline considered more important, like discussing the voting process or explaining the electoral college.

I'd learned that about Free Time—it wasn't really free. Just like our freedom. And there was hardly any time. At this rate, I wouldn't have half a book done by end of summer. So far, *Summer Lost & Reborn* was turning out to be *Summer Ignored & Incomplete*.

"Julia, it's thirty more minutes. We got this. You go first," Lizzie gave the order. Who died and made her Queen?

"Ugh, fine." I got into position between the starting cones.

"In three…two…one….go!" the girls cried in unison.

I took off toward the end cones, pumping my

legs as fast as they could go. The sooner we got this over with, the sooner we'd head back to the cabins and I could relax in the shade with an over-syrupy Sno Cone or icy wedge of watermelon. I heard the girls cheering me on, then realized why, even though it was just a qualifying run. In the lane next to me was Tinay, sprinting for her team. We were running against each other.

She was fast.

Of course, she was fast—she had the longest legs I'd ever seen on a girl, gazelle legs, but I was faster. No surprise. All my elementary school life, I'd been the fastest runner. I couldn't tell you how many times Coach Palermo wanted to put me on a county team to qualify for states, but I never wanted to do it. Sure, I was fast, but I didn't *enjoy* running, especially long distances. I didn't know how to breathe correctly. I always felt like my muscles were cramping up. Just because you had a natural talent for something didn't necessarily mean you *liked* doing it.

I crossed the invisible line stretching between the cones a solid second before Tinay reached hers, gasping for breath. As I made my way back to the group, Lizzie cried out, "Eight-point-five seconds!" holding up the stopwatch.

Tinay skulked off to find water.

Uleili took off after me. Lizzie timed her as well. She came in at 9.5 seconds, while Frances came in at a paltry 11 seconds. Without Lizzie running, I already knew I was the fastest in our group. Lizzie lined us up in order. She appointed herself the first leg, the other two in the middle, and I was assigned anchor.

"Please don't make me anchor," I begged.

"Why not?"

"I don't like the pressure."

"Julia, the fastest one goes last. That's how it's always been."

"But then everyone watches you, places their bets on you. You're expected to win, even if your team is behind. Trust me, I know. I always get chosen for field day, and I don't like running. I don't even like the sun. I don't even like batons. And let's not even get started on grass."

Lizzie frowned. "You're being a baby."

"Let Uleili go last. She was fast, too."

"Julia, you were the fastest one, so you go last. Those are the rules," Lizzie said, like the matter was over.

A little irked feeling started in my gut. "What rules? There are no rules. We're doing this for fun. Ms. Caroline even said to enjoy ourselves, not push too hard, since it's hot outside."

"So, you want us to lose against the other teams?" she asked.

"I never said that. I only said we don't have to be so serious about it. It's just a game."

"I know it's a game, but this is how it's done."

"Lizzie, why are you making such a big fuss about this? You're giving off strong dictatorship vibes here."

"What?" she scoffed. "I don't know why you're resisting for no reason. Do you not want to be anchor because you don't want to go up against Tinay? You know you already beat her once, right?"

"It's not because of that."

Granted, I was easily intimidated by Tinay and

shuddered to think the sass I'd get from her the rest of the day if I beat her in the relay races, but my trepidation wasn't because of that. I just didn't want to be the center of attention. And yes, maybe I was resisting Lizzie's "leadership" a bit.

Lizzie pulled me away until we were a safe distance from the other girls. "Why are you being difficult about this? What is the big hairy deal about being anchor?" She was on the verge of fuming. Either that or the summer heat was turning to steam inside her head.

"I'm not. I just don't like when you throw me into situations without warning."

"I'm not *throwing* you into anything, Julia. You were the fastest runner, and that automatically means that—"

"See? This is what I'm talking about. You think you're my coach, my drama teacher, the boss of everything. I don't like being thrown into a ring without warning. I want to choose for myself."

"But if I let you choose for yourself, you'd never do it." Her blue-eyed gaze bore into mine.

"What's that supposed to mean?"

"It means…" I could see it in her trembling lip. She thought I was a coward. She thought I was scared to do things at camp and was about to let me have it. "It means you don't take risks."

Dang.

Bullets to my soul.

I crossed my arms. "So, if I don't take risks the way you want me to take them, you're going to *make* me take them? Is that it?"

"If I don't make you do stuff, you won't do

anything."

I didn't like the tightness in my stomach during this argument. I didn't like feeling like I was caught between the truth and having to stand up for myself. Worse was feeling like I was about to lose the only person I cared about at camp. The world, even. But I also wasn't known for letting myself be coerced into a corner.

"I don't need a manager, Lizzie. And you're not my mom. You don't need to make decisions for me. Ever since we got to camp, you've been ordering me around. Just let me decide what I want. Even Ms. Caroline isn't forcing me into anything like you are."

"I have not been ordering you around." She crossed her arms.

"Fine, maybe not ordering, but herding me around like a sheep," I said.

And I could see a thought forming in her frontal lobe. *Because you act like a lost little sheep.* She didn't need to say it—I knew how Lizzie's mind worked. If you weren't clearly for or against something, she considered you lost, in need of direction, the perfect guinea pig for a Miss Bossypants.

"Fine, I'm not ordering you, or herding you," she said. "I'm asking you. As your friend."

"That's different. I'll run when I'm ready. The more you force me, the more I'll resist."

"Fine." Then, she sighed and let go of her crossed arms. "I'm sorry I want people to like you."

"I don't care if people like me." I trudged to the sidelines.

Yes, I wanted to win, but on my own terms. Ever since we got to camp, Lizzie had been throwing

me into uncomfortable situations when she knew—
knew—how I felt about it. Did she even care about me?
Or was this all about her need to arrange the Legos into
whatever shape she wanted? We weren't little kids
anymore.

The whistle blew, and CIT Patty barked through
her megaphone that we all had two minutes to put our
teams together, then the races would begin—first the 7-
8 year old group, then the 9-10s, then the 11-12s, and so
on up through 16, the age-out year. As anchor, I'd be up
against Tinay (for real this time). Foot planted up
against a tree, she stretched while giving me looks to
size me up.

I felt faint as I watched the other age groups
race. Lizzie offered me a water bottle, but I refused it. If
I drank water now, it would hit my stomach like a
brick.

Finally, it was time for our group. The whistle
blew again, CIT Patty calling us to our marks. Mine
was on the other side of the track, the last 100 yards.
The sun beat down on my forehead so hard, I'd have
sunburn before the end of the race. I got to my mark
and waited. Cheers wafted across the field, but I felt far
removed from the races, like I was operating using
someone else's body.

Tinay arrived with two other anchors. "Good
luck," she said to me.

"You, too," I said. My stomach hurt. Really
hurt. I wasn't sure I could do this. I could almost feel
everyone's anticipation, wagers, and hopes from across
the field. I wiped sweat off my brow with the edge of
my shirt.

"Your face is all pink," another girl said to me.

"Yeah, it's hot," I replied.

The whistle blew, long and loud. And they were off. I watched Lizzie run as fast as she could, pumping her arms with the silver baton in her hand. Already, she was behind the others. "Come on, Lizzie," I mumbled, watching her struggle. Finally, after a hundred yards, she reached Frances who got a running start while reaching back for the baton. They were off, sprinting faster than Lizzie.

Frances' legs moved like a blur. They were able to pass the two other teams. By the time Frances reached Uleili, the three teams were nearly tied. So yeah, that basically meant it'd be down to me, Tinay, and these other two girls. Great, just what I loved— attention and pressure.

My stomach crunched.

Uleili ran her hardest. On her face, I could see all her little hope eggs being placed into my basket. I took my cue and began a slow jog to receive the baton, looking forward while reaching back to feel for the solid object in my hand. Tinay did the same, her fingers twiddling like she was ready. Ready to kick my ass. My head pounded so hard, for a second, I saw the edges of my peripheral vision turn black.

Finally, I felt Uleili's breath behind my head and the smooth metal baton in my hand.

I shot off like a rocket.

Couldn't figure out which way so I followed Tinay who was a few inches ahead of me. If it weren't for her, I wouldn't have known which direction to point myself. My surrounding vision closed in. Cheers grew louder. Everyone jumped up and down from the sidelines. Even amongst the voices, my brain could pick out Lizzie's louder than the rest. "Come on, Julia! Yeah, come on, girl!"

Everyone else seemed to be cheering, "Tinay! Tinay!" and that threw my game off for a second, as I stumbled over my own foot and regained traction. They hated me. It was my own fault everyone hated me, I knew that, but now wasn't the time to let it bother me. I was neck and neck with Tinay, so close I could hear the airy rush of her ragged breaths. I did my best to keep up with her, and though I'd run faster than her during the practice round, I knew she was better off, because she wanted it more whereas I was only doing this to please Liz. My feet pounded the ground in uneven paces. My knees felt like they would buckle underneath me.

It was boiling—so hot outside. I couldn't see the finish line. I couldn't even see the track. All I knew was that I tripped, my feet flying out from underneath me, grass rushing toward me, scraping my cheek, earthy dirt smearing my face, and me thinking how sweet and good it smelled, but I was done. Eyes closed.

There were cheers.

There were shouts. *Is she okay? Julia!*

And then there was nothing.

TEN

I heard her voice before I saw her—a woman speaking gently, quietly, into a wrist phone. "She's fine. She's resting. Yes...no...yes, I'll make sure she does."

My eyes fluttered open. From the shadows on the wall, I figured it was getting to be late afternoon. She stood against the nurse's station wall, staring out the window at girls playing outside. They screeched and laughed, same as they had in my dreams. When the woman in white shorts and light green polo glanced at me and found me watching her, she floated over.

"You okay?"

"What happened?" I mumbled.

"You fainted out on the field. We carried you here. You don't remember?"

Bits and pieces. "I remembered fainting. Then I woke up."

"That's right. You confirmed your name, said you were tired, so that was good, but we brought you here where you've been sleeping for an hour. I'm Nurse Annelle, by the way. I've been keeping an eye on you."

"Who won?" I asked, sitting up.

"Excuse me?"

My head thrummed. "Who won the race? The relay race."

Nurse Annelle laughed. "Still stuck on that, huh? I have no idea. Here, drink some more." She handed me a sports drink bottle halfway full of clear liquid. It was sweet and tasted like citrus. "You're slightly overheated, Julia. Ms. Caroline wants you to stay in here for a while until your temperature is down. It's a little elevated, but your pulse looks great. Do you need to use the bathroom yet?"

"No."

"Okay, keep drinking. I'll be back in a few to check on you. Are you comfortable?"

I nodded.

"Good." Nurse Annelle patted me on the shoulder, waited while I took another few sips of the sports drink, then walked out. "I'm going to leave the door open so you can catch a breeze." She left, as the door swung back and forth on its hinges.

I lay there, staring at the wooden beams cross the ceiling, the dark, old cabinets against the wall, counters with various objects strewn across them. Bandages, gauze pads, alcohol prep pads. Four walls containing me. Sun streaming through the window. Warm, summer breezes felt better than the direct heat had earlier, but I knew of a cooler, more shady place to relax. I finished the sports drink bottle, then snuck out before she could return.

Taking the shortcuts to the woods, I made a beeline for the Writer's Hut and slipped inside. There, I plopped myself on the couch by the window. I stared at the hanging lantern, encased in a few strands of spider silk, at the American flag quilt on the wall. These objects felt like companions, good ol' friends. I'd have been lying if I said I wanted to be outside with the other girls. The truth was, I felt safer here overall than anywhere else. I was scared of what the girls would say (or were saying already) about me, even though I knew Lizzie would defend me if it came down to it.

After a while of decompressing, I stood and stretched my achy muscles, moved to the desk, and ran my fingers along the wood. If I was required to rest, I may as well take advantage, try and write a few more pages. Pulling out the chair, I plopped onto the cushion and waited for the computer to wake up.

"Hello, Julia. Ready to write another chapter of *Summer Lost & Reborn*?" it asked, the glowing screen of the vintage typewriter's fake paper coming to life. "It's been a few days."

"I may as well. I'm stuck."

"Stuck is good. Let's stretch your imagination, shall we?" The computer scanned my bio and pulled up my story, right where I last left it. "Would you like me to read the last page where you left off?"

"No, thanks. I can take it from here."

"Very well. Happy writing!"

"Happy...computing."

"Thank you!" it said, as though computers were unappreciated these days.

I had my next scene all worked out in my head, but I also wanted to write about today's experience. Needed to, to get it off my chest. The pressure, the friendship with Lizzie, my inability to unblock my fear. It made sense to write about the races, the tension with my best friend, and why I couldn't bring myself to show off my full potential, like she wanted me to. What was holding me back?

I'd only gotten a few paragraphs in and I was

feeling pretty good about letting the creative juices flow again, when there was a knock at the door. I quickly spun in the chair, ready to defend why I'd left the nurses' station, in case it was Nurse Annelle hunting me down.

Lizzie wafted into the room. "Hey. How're you feeling?" She sat on the edge of the dirty old couch, as if afraid to commit to an entire sitting position.

"Fine. They said I passed out."

She nodded. "It was scary. You were a couple feet from the finish line when you collapsed."

"I take it I didn't win."

She pressed her lips together. "Tinay did."

My chest tightened. "I figured. Well, I told you I couldn't do it. Did my best."

Lizzie stared at me with those big gray-blue eyes of hers. She had a thin smile that was hard to read, unlike the usual peppy Lizzie smile, and her hands were clasped in her lap. "Julia."

"What?"

"I don't know how to say this, but…"

I raised my eyebrows. "We always said we could say anything to each other."

She nodded, her cheeks relaxing a bit. "Yeah. You're right. Okay. I'm just going to say it. I…I feel like…like maybe you made yourself sick. Does that make sense?"

My eyebrows twisted into a knot. "Huh? You think I got sick on purpose? Like, to lose the race?"

"No, no, of course not. What I mean is…a person's negativity can make them sick. Haven't you ever heard of that?"

"I'm not that negative, Lizzie."

"I think you are. I think your fear of doing stuff, of talking in public or being around people, or fear of people watching you sends a signal from your brain to your body that you're stressed, and your body reacts like there's something wrong, and—"

I shot up, nearly knocking the chair down. "I can't believe what I'm hearing."

"It's called neuroplasticity, Julia. We learned about it in school. You can look it up if you don't believe me."

"It's called a heat stroke, Lizzie," I rose my voice then began pacing the cabin. "It's almost a hundred freakin' degrees outside today."

"Okay, but what about the other times? What about when you walk away from the campfire when we're trading stories, or when you're picked for a part?"

"I'm shy, Lizzie. My god, what don't you get? Not everybody is like you."

"You don't have to be."

"That's what you want. You want me to be like you. Well, I'm not. You're going to have to understand that not everyone is Miss Perfect, daughter of Mrs. Idealistic."

"What does that mean?" She bristled with hurt in her eyes.

"What it means is…never mind. Look, I didn't lose on purpose. I just got heat stroke. I would've finished the race if I hadn't gotten sick."

"But you weren't even running as fast as I've seen you run before, and that's what I'm talking about. I want people to see the Julia I see. I want you to shine. Is that such a bad thing? You're acting like it's a bad thing, and I care about you."

"You sure you care about me? Or do you want to take credit for turning me into someone I'm not?" I crossed my arms and waited while she stopped faking a stinging feeling.

"What?" She stood, confusion all over your face. "Look, all I'm saying is if you think negatively, it affects you negatively. You have to think positively for things to work out, and if you don't start doing that, I'm worried you'll always be sick. I'm worried about what else could happen to you. Today it's heat stroke. But tomorrow?"

"You seriously believe I'm making myself sick?"

"Yes, I do. Negativity affects your whole worldview."

"So, you think positively…all the time?" I asked her incredulously.

"I try to. I'm not saying it always works. Jules, you know this is true. Your mom has been saying this all your life."

"That doesn't mean it's true. It's like saying God or Jesus really exist in the world, or aliens are orbiting out planet right now. We can believe it until we're blue in the face, but it doesn't mean there's any proof."

She sat back, staring at me. "I can't believe you just said that," she said quietly.

"I…" Maybe I'd never said it out loud. But I was twelve years old and a lot of the things I'd always taken as fact as a kid, I wasn't sure what to think of now. "I can't believe you're trying to make me feel bad for getting sick!" I shouted.

She sighed, threw her hands up. "I don't even know who you are right now, like who I'm talking to. You don't sound like Julia."

"And you don't sound like the Lizzie."

"Maybe I'm a different person here. Look, I don't want to fight. I just came in here to tell you...well, what I thought...but now I see that was a mistake."

"Maybe you should've considered what you were going to say before you came in here and said it. You're not the expert on everything," I told her.

"Trust me, I did consider it. I thought I could trust my best friend, my cousin, to listen without getting all defensive. Guess I was wrong."

"I wouldn't have to get defensive if you wouldn't keep attacking me! Just let me be myself!" I stormed outside. I had to use the bathroom anyway, a fact that would please Nurse Annelle and Ms. Caroline, because after all, a solid pee when dehydrated was a good sign.

Lizzie followed me out. "Julia, you know how I know these things exist without proof?"

I slowed and turned to her, hands on my hips. "How?"

"It's called faith. And you could use some of it right now." She turned and headed back to the cabins, just as the whistle blew and all the girls started heading back as well.

Great. My only friend was mad at me.

But she started it.

I used the bathroom, went back to tell Nurse Annelle where I was, that I was fine, and asked Ms. Caroline if I could stay in the Writer's Hut the rest of the day, because writing was making me feel better and I could use the recovery time. With adults, how you painted a situation was everything. She agreed, said all I needed to do was check in with her every so often, and called me a "world-famous author" once again.

I smiled as I left, but as my footsteps made their way back to the cabin, the smile melted away. The feeling of being physically exhausted had left me, but in its place was an emotional exhaustion. My heart ached. The world was not as it should be if Lizzie was mad at me.

Still, I got what I wanted—the rest of the day in the Writer's Hut, typing away to my heart's delight, transforming everything that had happened that day into narrative. Private words that would one day be shared. Right now, they were still mine, moldable like Play-Doh, but one day, people would read them. I might get awards, recognition, maybe even money. I tried to ✝ sound advanced, mature, when writing, because no one would take me seriously otherwise, but I also tried to sound my age so people could remark, "What a lovely young author, that Julia Weissman, writing with such maturity for her age."

When I was done hours later, I sat back feeling super accomplished. The sky was now dark, as stars twinkled high above the moonless night over Lake Bradford. From out of the woods toward the warm glow of the cabins, I could hear girls singing around the campfire, hear laughter, and feel the forever friendships being made out there.

So, why, if I valued that so much, was I inside an isolated hut, writing about it instead of experiencing it for myself? Why couldn't I get out there and make friends like Lizzie wanted me to? Maybe I did have a problem. Maybe I was too negative, like she said. Maybe our bodies did respond to what our brains told them, and because I was afraid of social interaction, mine was ordering my body to be alone.

Because here I was alone. Listening to campfire songs from a hundred yards away. By myself. Just like I wanted.

ELEVEN

"I've caught up to you. Now you can't make fun of me for being younger than you anymore." Lizzie said that to me every year on her birthday whenever Ms. Caroline was nice enough to let us talk to her via hologram.

Because Elizabeth's birthday fell on July 4th every year, I hadn't been able to spend it with her in four years. She'd been at Camp Auctus every one of them. How cool was that, to have fireworks set off in your honor? Lucky.

"You're officially twelve now. *Way* more mature than eleven," I joked, tossing a rock into the lake. "Oh, by the way, I made you something." Pulling the folded aqua sheet of tissue from my pocket, I presented her with the greatest gift there ever was.

"A handmade gift from Julia?" She patted her heart. "Wow, I'm super honored."

"Sarcasm doesn't suit you."

"No, I mean it. Whenever you make something, it's always perfect, like a professional artisan made it. Let's see if you outdid yourself this time. You know how I feel about the little box you decoupaged for me."

For the holidays last year, I'd made her a painted box with her name on it made from cut-out letters in different fonts. She kept it on her desk in her room filled with lucky items she found on her dog walks. I always felt she really treasured it. Lizzie was good at treasuring other people's talents.

We were sitting by the lake with the rest of the camp, administrators, CITs, and counselors. Everybody either played volleyball, dressed as founding mothers using costumes from the drama department, sang, talked, or swirled sparklers in big circles in the evening light, signing their names in the air. A quarter moon sat high in the sky, and something magically ethereal lit the night. I always felt that way on Independence Day, like floating through a timeless dream.

Even more so today, because we were at camp together for the first time, and though I had to share Lizzie on her birthday with dozens of her friends, it still felt special. At least I was here with her.

I waited with anticipation, as she unwrapped the folded tissue. Inside the square nest were two charms I'd made in Arts & Crafts made of polymer clay. I'd painted them white and blue with sparkles over an iridescent sheen. But the fun part about it, when you put them together, they made a heart. Half of it said BE FRI and the other half said ST ENDS.

"Oh," she exclaimed, holding the pieces up to the light.

"I got the idea from Grandma Wendy," I explained. "One time, at her house, she showed me—"

"The gold BEST FRIENDS charm she and her best friend shared when they were little," she guessed. "It was trendy back in the 1980s."

"Yes!"

"She told me about it too, and I always thought

that idea was so cool!"

"I know, me too! Here, you take BE FRI, and I'll take ST ENDS." Each half of the heart had its own little metal loop, and we each got a black cord to go with it. I took my half, held it up, so she would "toast" with me. "Happy Birthday to my best friend in the whole world. Thank you for making me come to camp with you. You're right, sometimes I need a good kick in the butt."

"Oh, Julia." She hugged me tightly. "I know I can be bossy. I'm sorry."

"You're not," I said, my cheek against her hair. Her skin smelled of coconutty sun protection. "That's what family is for." We laced our necklaces around our necks and gave each other high fives.

"Hey, I have an idea." With a thumb, she felt the smoothness of the charm hanging from her neck. "When we go home, before seventh grade starts, let's do something fun, something together."

"Like what?"

"I don't know. I was thinking a video series or something. We could call it *Liz & Jules*. I give life advice to kids our age, and maybe you do book reviews. We can figure it out. It can be anything, as long as we do it together. What do you think?"

"It sounds amazing, but you know I'm not going to be good at it."

"See, that's just it, Jules. Because it's only the two of us, you won't have an actual audience. Only you, me, and our channel. It could help you get over your fear of talking in front of people, and you can pick whatever topic you like. Sometimes, we can pick topics out of a hat. Whatever, I think it could be fun."

"Okay, let's do it. We'll have to figure out our looks. You're the blonde one, I'm the brunette, obviously, but there should be more. Like two different fashion styles entirely, two different ways of thinking…we can even handle tough topics facing people today."

"See? Now you're getting it. That's what I'm talking about—a channel to get people realizing that we don't always have to agree on everything, but we can still respect each other's opinions. Let's plan it the rest of our time here at camp, and then figure out when we want to start."

"Okay." I smiled. Oddly enough, I was excited about this. Like she said, there'd be no actual audience, so I might not feel as nervous, and it might help me get over this whole super-introvert thing.

We heard the screech of the microphone and saw Ms. Caroline getting ready to make an announcement. The whole camp broke into applause when she held her hands up in the air and said, "Are we having a great time tonight?"

Cheers erupted in waves across the lakeside, as paper lanterns bobbed over the stage in the delicious summer breeze.

"Good, I am so glad. Are you all loving this barbecue as much as I am?"

More cheers and whistles.

"Excellent. Don't forget to thank the mess hall staff and all our volunteers. They've been working hard all day to make this 4th of July feast the best it can be for you all. I hope you've all written down at least three things about our nation you're grateful for for the time capsule we're doing this year, and don't forget, if you're planning on performing in the Talent Extravaganza, you have to sign up by tomorrow afternoon. And now, speaking of tomorrow afternoon, I have a special surprise for you all."

Lizzie and I looked at each other and laughed privately. Ms. Caroline was always saying she had a "special surprise" for us, then it turned out to be a guest speaker nobody knew, or freshly made T-shirts we all had to wear, or a new flavor of muffin in the breakfast buffet.

"We have a guest speaker coming..."

Lizzie and I exchanged looks again, stifling more giggles.

But there was something about the way Ms. Caroline was saying it this time, I almost felt like she was looking for us, as she scanned the grounds with her neck stretched out, and those bright eyes searched. "We will meet in the amphitheater after breakfast tomorrow promptly at 10 AM. You all know her as the woman putting together an exploratory committee, she's declared her intention to run for President, she's esteemed Camp Auctus alumni, *and* the mother of one of our very own campers..."

I knew it.

"...we are so excited to have U.S. Senator Emma Singletary-Richards from Florida visiting us here tomorrow!"

I turned to Lizzie and took my clues from whatever expression appeared on her face. If she smiled mischievously, then she already knew this sparkling turn of events. Instead, her jaw dropped and she screamed. "My mom! My mom is coming!" Lizzie shot up, pulling me to my feet with her, and hugged me.

Then, she did a little dance.

I wasn't happy that all eyes were on us, but I was definitely happy for Lizzie.

Everyone broke into applause, including Ms. Caroline onstage. "I am very glad to hear that reaction, Miss Elizabeth." The adults all seemed to find that one funny and broke into chuckles.

"That's so amazing," I said, shaking her hands out. "Aunt Emma is coming. Yay! Did you know?"

"I had no clue. She must've taken a different route on her campaign trail. I thought she was going to be in New York this week. Oh, my God, I'm like in shock."

"She probably wanted to surprise you for your birthday," I said.

Most people wouldn't freak out so much if they discovered their mother was coming to visit them at their social studies camp like this, but Lizzie was different. Aunt Emma was different. I knew they hadn't had much time together this year like most mother-daughters, so I was genuinely happy for her.

As if to punctuate the news, another round of fireworks went off, illuminating the night sky over Lake Bradford like one million fireflies dancing just for Lizzie's birthday. I smiled big, because I was finally here to see it.

TWELVE

My aunt, Emma, was the grownup version of Lizzie with her long blonde hair, blue eyes, and total confidence in herself. Seeing her always made me feel positively happy for the rest of the day. It made sense that people everywhere loved her. When she walked into the amphitheater's backstage area that morning, escorted by Ms. Caroline and her own security team, it was like seeing a celebrity instead of a family member.

Lizzie jumped from the bench and ran into her mother's arms. "Mom!"

I immediately got secondhand warm fuzzies just watching their reunion and waited a few seconds so they could enjoy their own hug without me. But Aunt Emma extended her reach and pulled me in, like a free-floating space particle getting sucked into Earth's orbit.

"Girls! I've missed you so much!" she cried.

I felt every ounce of her love. Through her sigh, I could sense how draining it'd been for her on the road and seeing us was like recharging her empty battery.

Ms. Caroline tiptoed near us with her clipboard and pen, which meant the activities must keep running. "Okay, girls. Go take your seats. The Senator will give her speech, and then you'll reunite for plenty of chit chat afterwards. I promise!" She skedaddled Lizzie and me, but prying Lizzie off her mother wasn't easy.

Aunt Emma laughed, unfazed by Ms. Caroline's order, and clung tight to Lizzie. "Okay, baby. You heard Ms. Caroline. Go ahead and we'll see each other afterwards. I'm not going anywhere."

"Fine, but don't start answering adult questions about the issues before me. I get you first."

"You first—always." Aunt Emma waved at us, as we walked around the side into the amphitheater already buzzing with people clapping and chanting in expectation of my aunt's appearance. Even though she was just a Senator from Florida, she was already a lot of the country's favorite presidential candidate, because she was smart and pretty young, and even kids knew everything about her.

"Is she there? Is she wearing Shrimp?" Cassie asked. Pics of Aunt Emma had been circulating around social media of her wearing this super cute pink flamingo pin on her blouse she named Shrimp because of what flamingoes eat. Also, because…Florida.

"Yes, she's wearing Shrimp," I answered proudly, since I was in Senator Emma's inner circle— her family circle—and I could answer questions about her like that.

The girls craning their necks in the first row to hear us report about the Senator sat back, as Ms. Caroline came onstage to cheers and hollers. She tapped the microphone and waited until the girls' chatter died down. "Camp Auctus! Are you ready for our special guest?"

The whole amphitheater broke into louder cheers and applause. Next to me, Lizzie bounced in her seat. Anyone watching her face could see the sheer amount of pride splashed all over it.

"Let's welcome Florida Senator Emma Singletary-Richards!" One of the counselors played Hail to the Chief on the speaker, the same song used for Presidents of the United States whenever they stepped onto a stage, and even though I was used to hearing my aunt be introduced in public settings, this time felt more special somehow.

My aunt walked onto the stage, wearing a green Camp Auctus T-shirt over her white blouse. She stepped up to the microphone and paused for a quick photo with Ms. Caroline before speaking. "Thank you, everyone. I am so excited to be back on my old stomping grounds. I don't get to make it every year when Lizzie starts camp, so I'm really thrilled to be here."

She went on to say how being on the campaign trail has been fun. She's gotten to meet a lot of different people from all around the U.S. but how nothing feels as great as coming home to family, and Camp Auctus has always felt like one of her first families. She added that Lizzie was one of her driving forces, that whenever she formed an opinion on a topic, she always thought about how it would affect her daughter's future. Lizzie was her guidepost, her lighthouse, her beacon.

"And my niece, too," she added for my benefit to some chuckles through the venue. "Love you guys. They're always together, those two."

"Oh, my God." I felt my face flush.

Lizzie patted me on the knee. "Now you know how I feel."

Aunt Emma went on to talk about Separation of Powers and Checks and Balances in our government.

My brain and eyes started going numb. This always happened when someone started talking about something I didn't quite get or maybe thought was complicated. She went on to explain that Separation of Powers is how our government is divided into three branches: Executive, Legislative, and Judicial. Checks and Balances is the power each branch has to "check" or limit the other branches, which helps us maintain a balance of power by insuring one branch cannot have absolute power.

Honestly, this was not helping. We'd had a big breakfast, and I was ready to start dozing.

Just then, she turned and focused her eyes on Lizzie and me. Immediately, I sat a little more upright in my chair, and I sensed Lizzie do the same.

"This is a crucial fabric of our country. You must be skeptical and leery of anyone who suggests abandoning these foundations." Aunt Emma let out a sigh. "Thousands of years of history and millions and millions of deaths have reaffirmed their necessity."

Millions of deaths? *Okay, fine,* I thought, *you got my attention.*

"There is something I call being tribal. It was a term shared with me when I was your age. It's when a group of people, a tribe, believes that only it knows the right way forward. Our group is right, and everyone else is wrong. This is a dangerous way of thinking, ladies."

I got where she was coming from. I personally felt we should always have an Apple Brown Betty with ice cream on Friday nights, and anyone who thought otherwise was clearly wrong and should be thrown into the lake. But I knew she was talking about more serious stuff.

"Anytime there is a debate between groups, it is too easy to start thinking of the merits of 'being tribal,' that there should only be one voice, and the shared purpose we believe at the moment is the absolute right one, and anyone who disagrees must be mentally ill. It all depends on where you stand, what life has been like for you. That's why it's important to have empathy."

Wasn't this getting a little too intense for summer camp?

I looked at Lizzie but she was focused on her mom.

"There are many pitfalls that come with thinking this way. You become a listener who can only hear your own group's voice, and it starts to become very easy to believe the little lies that your tribal leader has been saying. And they repeat those lies over and over until you think well, they must be true, right? And eventually the lies get bigger and bigger as the group gets used to believing whatever the leader says, because it's just easier that way."

What she said seemed to make sense. The more opinions we listened to, the better full picture of the truth we'd have.

"Sounds crazy, right?" She raised her hands in a display of disbelief and panned the audience. "All you have to do is look around at the headlines of the world's news outlets. There are plenty of leaders who tell their followers that only they are right, and everyone who suggests differently is societal poison. And those leaders will do anything to convince their members to keep moving into the darkness because that is the only thing that keeps them in power. They breed paranoia, suspicion, and fear, which always leads to hate."

She paused, and I realized I had started to grip my seat pretty hard. I relaxed my hands and took in a breath. When I thought about it, I could identify a few "leaders" who behaved like this. So was the right thing to do to listen to as many leaders as possible?

"Just remember this, be skeptical of any leader who suggests that the only thing keeping them from making things better is people with other viewpoints, to believe only what they say, and that if only they had the power without interference, only then can they fulfill their promise and make the world better."

She took another breath, and then in a quicker, more exuberant manner, added, "Every person throughout human history who's spouted this rhetoric is dangerous."

"We have the responsibility to keep our nation great by growing, improving, and evolving. Always remember, different viewpoints are important, debate is crucial, your vote is precious, and without participation, democracy falls apart."

There were cheers but also, when I looked around to see how people responded to my aunt, a few rolled their eyes, which I didn't understand. Ugh, why did things have to be complicated? It was a good speech. It turned out more interesting than I thought it would.

When she was done with the Q&A, she said goodbye and the whole place stood and cheered. My heart felt full just knowing she was my aunt who'd be going through so many sacrifices to ensure our voices were heard. Being a politician wasn't easy but she made it seem easy, because she did it so well.

Afterwards, it was free time all over campus, as food tents went up, as they always did whenever we had a special guest. Basically, it was 4th of July, Part Two, with the barbecue, races, games, and party atmosphere.

"Let's go find my mom," Lizzie said, grabbing me by the arm and heading toward the big tent where camp administrators were going all out for Aunt Emma.

We found her listening and nodding in front of Ms. Caroline and a few others, sipping on lemonade and fanning herself with an official Camp Auctus Guest Speaker program. Her eyes lit up when she saw us, and I loved how she said, "Excuse me, Ms. Caroline. I made a promise and a promise I shall keep," butting out of the small crowd to single out Lizzie and me.

"You were great, Aunt Emma," I said.

She hugged my shoulders. "Oh, thank you, Jules! Believe it or not, I never get fully used to it. I still get nervous."

"See?" Lizzie's eyes widened to me. "Even she gets nervous around people."

It couldn't be true, but my aunt nodded. "Oh, yeah. Always, before I speak to a crowd. But you know what? I always remember that I'm here to listen to people, talk about the things that matter to them, and provide solutions, so I'm already in a safe space. Not always—debates can get ugly—but I just breathe through it. Like your mom taught me," she said to me. "She's always so good at staying calm."

I wasn't sure I could agree with that assessment of my mom, but I was sure Aunt Emma thought so because my mother loved taking and teaching yoga classes where meditation was a big focus.

"Anyway, I have a question for you, my love," she said to Lizzie, pulling her aside. I hung back awkwardly, not sure if the private meeting was meant for my ears or not. "I was thinking, since you're older now and this is an especially challenging year for us, would you want to come on the road with me?"

Lizzie's jaw dropped. "When? Right now?"

Aunt Emma laughed. "Well, not right now-now. But tomorrow, when I leave. Would you like to come on the campaign trail with me? I know you'd probably rather stay here with Julia, and Camp Auctus is way more fun than a boring campaign trail, but..."

"Are you serious?"

"Yes, Elizabeth, I'm serious. I haven't gotten to see much of you the last few months, and I miss my little monkey."

Lizzie hugged her mother around the waist, and I could already feel a lead balloon sinking to the ground, falling fast. "Mommy, I'd love to go. Are you sure I can? I don't have to stay here?"

Have to? What about me?

"You would have to take it seriously. I'd be busy working, but in between rallies and important dinners, we could have girl time. What do you think?" Did she mean to take Lizzie but not me? Would I even want to go if she asked me to come along, too? Aunt Emma glanced at me. "Julia, I would ask you as well, but your mom already said she wants you to stay here."

"She did?" I asked.

"Yes, I wanted to know what she thought before I brought it up. She said she wanted you to have the full Camp Auctus experience at least one whole summer the way we all have. And I agree. Every girl in our family should have it, and this being your first year—"

"I don't want to go," I blurted.

It was true—I didn't. There was nothing appealing to me about tagging along with Aunt Emma from state to state hearing her same campaign speech over and over, meeting new people, talking to people, and being nothing but sociable. No, thanks. At least here I had my Writer's Hut, my solitude whenever I wanted.

"You can go if you want," I told Lizzie.

Then I walked away.

Because I didn't want to be standing there when Lizzie chose her mother over hanging with me the rest of the summer. She missed her so much, there was no doubt I was about to get discarded like yesterday's meatloaf. There was no doubt where I was headed either, without lunch, without another word. Straight to the Julia Isolation Hut, a.k.a. the Writer's Hut, holding my breath the whole way. She'd asked me to come to Camp Auctus so I could experience a quintessential tradition, but I was about to experience it alone.

When I got to the hut, I slammed the door shut and threw myself onto the couch, letting go of the air my lungs weren't able to breathe. Then I broke into tears.

THIRTEEN

For the rest of the day, Lizzie bounced back and forth between coming to find me at the Writer's Hut, lakeside, campfire, or mess hall and spending time with her mom. It was like she couldn't decide who she wanted to be with more, who she loved more. It wasn't fair to think that way, but it was how it felt.

The truth was, I already knew Lizzie's decision and didn't want to feel any more hurt than I already was. I couldn't blame her. I mean, of course she wanted to be with her mom. On the other hand, I was mad at Aunt Emma. Why did she have to take my cousin away? But I had no right to be upset at either of them. If Aunt Emma wanted to spend time with her daughter, she was allowed to.

I mean, she *gave birth* to her.

Before dinner, Aunt Emma tried talking to me herself. "Hey, famous author," she said, knocking on the door to the Writer's Hut. "Hope I'm not interrupting the flow of words."

She was.

"Julia, honey…are you mad at me?"

I was.

She came in and stood there. I could feel her behind me like a ghost.

"I know you are. That's a silly question." She took a seat on the edge of the couch, just like her daughter always did. "Honey, it'll only be for a couple of weeks. I'll send her back if she gets bored or wants to return. You know Lizzie, she'll want to come back to you. She always wants to be with you."

"Not this time, she doesn't," I mumbled.

Her sigh was like a hurricane wind, but I held fast like a palm tree. "It's complicated, Julia. I rarely see her anymore. It's so hard doing my job and not getting to see my daughter. I would bring you along, too. I told you I tried…" She scooted closer to the end of the couch, so she could see my face, since I was trying hard to hide it with my hair. "But your mom wants you to stay here."

"It's fine. I understand."

It wasn't fine. I didn't understand.

"Well…I can see I'm interrupting your work," she said and stood. "What are you writing anyway?"

"A novel."

"You amaze me, Julia. You really do. I'm forty years old, and I've still never written a full book. You take after your amazing mom."

She was only trying to butter me up, but I appreciated the kind words. "Thank you," I replied, giving her a quick look. "It's about friendship." In that one moment, I saw a tender smile, or maybe an apology, I wasn't sure.

"That's incredibly lovely. I'll get out of your hair so you can keep working." And she did. She left me alone, just like I wanted, and I never felt so sad to have someone leave my space.

I wanted to change my mind and tell her she

wasn't bothering me, but for some reason, I couldn't. I couldn't let it go or "get over it," like I knew my dad would tell me. He loved to say how the world didn't bend your way, and it was better to be flexible and learn to adjust to disappointments in life than to wish things were different.

But I wished things were different.

My sole reason for being here was leaving.

All through breakfast, I pretended to eat so it would look like I didn't care. If I cared, I wouldn't eat, so I ate all the muffins, all the fruit, and all the scrambled eggs, barely leaving enough for the rest of my cabin mates. I was the epitome of not caring! Lizzie didn't show up to breakfast anyway, so she didn't get to witness my not caring. She was busy getting packed up to leave, so her mom's security guys could carry all her stuff away and leave an empty bunk where there used to be an Elizabeth.

The other girls knew something was wrong, because they kept asking, "Are you okay, Julia?" But I would just nod, smile, and drink my orange juice, because of course I was okay. WHY WOULDN'T I BE OKAY??

Ms. Caroline was walking down every aisle making sure we all swallowed our food, because "breakfast is the most important meal of the day, ladies!" It took all my willpower not to vomit on her shoes when she reached me. I knew that she knew that I knew that Lizzie was leaving with Aunt Emma this morning, that I was faking being totally fine with it, and perhaps the whole situation needed a Camp Auctus intervention.

"Miss Julia?" She crouched next to me. My fault for sitting at the end of the bench. Next time, I'd have to buffer my sides with Cassie or Tori.

"Yes, ma'am?" I looked up, a half-baked smile on my face.

"Can you come with me? When you're done with that bite, of course." She stood and held out her hand, as if I'd take it. Already, half the camp was watching me, and I wanted to tell Ms. Caroline she could stop with the dramatics now—she was making it all worse.

I collected the empty muffin liners, made a garbage ball, and put it on my tray. Then I stood and walked the tray to the trash bin, tossing out all the garbage and putting the tray on top of the bin. Ms. Caroline escorted me the whole way, as if I were a wild deer that might flee into the woods if given the chance.

"Am I in trouble?" I followed her out of the mess hall.

"Why would you be in trouble?"

Oh, I don't know. Because I've been cold and mean to everyone.

We reached her office, but we were only there so she could drop off her walkie-talkie, then we headed around the side to a small secluded garden in the back where Ms. Caroline sometimes sat alone in the middle of the day. The area doubled as playing field for the younger girls, but at the moment, it seemed empty from the lack of giggles. When we came around the corner, though, Lizzie was there, sitting on a bench.

She looked up, almost alarmed to see me.

Ms. Caroline smiled and wrung her hands nervously. "Oh! Is that Ms. Susan calling me? Oh, dear,

I think I'll leave you two alone for a minute. Be right back."

She wouldn't be right back. This had been a devious ploy to get us together so we could "talk" and "make up," and if Ms. Caroline thought *that* was going to happen, she had another thing coming.

"Hey," Lizzie chirped a small, sad sound. Maybe she'd decided not to go after all. She'd realized the errors of her ways in abandoning me at Camp Auctus after she'd invited me here to begin with, and we were here so she could apologize to me.

"Hey," I said.

"I didn't want to bother you in case you were in the Writer's Hut, so Ms. Caroline went and got you for me."

"That's okay."

"I just wanted to say goodbye."

Wait... Goodbye? "So, you're still leaving?"

"Of course, I am. You know I am. You heard my mom."

"I did hear your mom, but I also heard her ask you if you wanted to stay. She gave you a choice. You're still leaving?"

"I was always leaving, Julia. Look, I know you're not happy about this, but it's not the end of the world."

"It is to me!" I shouted. Dang, I'd totally blown my carefully rehearsed not-caring cover.

"I know. But I hardly ever see my mom anymore, and she's always saying how I'm too young to go with her anywhere, but for the first time in, ever, she asked me to come along. I have to go!"

"You don't have to."

"You're right—I want to go. I want to see what my mom does for a living. I want to be there with her when she gives speeches. I want to meet the citizens of this country and hear their problems, so my mom can fix them. I want this."

"Then, go. Nobody's stopping you." I turned to leave the garden.

She grabbed my hand. I shook out of her grasp. "I don't want you to be mad at me."

"You can't ask me not to be mad, Lizzie. I only came to Camp Auctus for you, and now you're abandoning me."

"You're not alone. You have Cassie, Tori, all the other girls…"

"I have no one, and you know it."

"Whose fault is that?" she asked. I felt like I'd been stung in the forehead by a sassy dart. "For weeks, I've been trying to get you to participate in stuff, but you always choose the Writer's Hut, the Writer's Hut, the Writer's Hut."

"Because I'm writing a book."

"Because you're scared of making friends. That was why I invited you here, Julia, and if I stay…if I hang around you, nobody *but* you, like you want me to…you'll never make friends."

"That's not true."

"It is," she said, approaching me. Since when was a recently-turned twelve-year-old allowed to exude the wisdom and ageless beauty of an adult? At that moment, I hated her for telling the truth. "You're using me as a crutch."

My jaw dropped. "Did you make that up yourself, or did your mom give you that one?" Fuming,

I turned my back to her and faced Ms. Caroline's rear window. Something fluttered behind the curtain.

"I knew you were going to react like this. That's why I wrote something for you. Ms. Caroline has it. You'll see. Maybe my leaving will be good. Hang out with Cassie. She's really nice."

"Not to me."

"Julia, that's because you don't give anyone a chance. People don't know what to think of you. You're like this cactus I keep telling everyone is actually not that prickly, if they just get to know you."

"Now I'm a cactus?"

"You know what I mean. They're nice girls. Just talk to them. They're just like you and me with dreams and hobbies and big, big plans for the future!" She smiled. "What if I can't always be with you? What if…I don't know…what if I have to move?"

"Why would you move? Your mom is Florida State Senator."

"The point is, I can't always be by your side. That doesn't mean I don't love you any less."

How could I argue with her when she beamed like that? I would forever and always envy Elizabeth's positivity and zest for life. The world did not deserve her.

I started crying. I hated myself for it, but I also couldn't stop it. Why did this feel so horrible when I knew it was only temporary? It wasn't like Lizzie was disappearing forever.

I wiped my face of ugly tears. "I'm going to call my mom and see if I can come home. If you're not staying, I don't want to stay either."

"Julia, just stay. Please? For me." She carefully

stepped up to me and opened her arms. Part of me wanted to run. I wouldn't accept this call that'd been made without me. But all of me wanted to hug her.

In the distance, I heard Aunt Emma calling for her.

This was it.

"I have to go. Stop being stubborn and hug me."

I leaned into her and let her put her arms around me, but I didn't hug her back. Rather, I let her hug me. "My sweet cousin," she said, pulling back and lifting the half of the heart around her chest—BE FRI. "Best friends forever? I'll see you at home when we get back. We'll do our video series then, okay? Start writing down ideas!"

I barely nodded. I was doing everything possible not to cry. I wanted to dissolve into a puddle on the floor, just seep into the grassy field and hide.

"I love you, Jules," she said. "I'll talk to you soon."

Say it. Say it or you'll regret it, something told me.

"I love you back, Elizabeth Richards."

She smiled big, which always made my heart lift, no matter how mad I felt inside. That was her biggest superpower. I watched her run off through the garden down the grassy path, golden ends of her hair flailing out behind her like the trail of pixie dust behind a really happy magical creature. I clutched the half a heart around my neck—my brokenhearted ST ENDS— and watched her leave until I couldn't see her anymore.

FOURTEEN

For the next week, I moped endlessly, yet the weirdest things made me happy.

Like the scent of pine trees wafting in through the cabin window. Or the afternoon rain, and the summery combo scents of sunscreen and humidity, which always put me in a melancholy mood. Toasted marshmallow and burning wood in the evenings. Every single smell reminded me of fun times with Lizzie. In the mornings, I kept bolting up in bed, though, excited for a new day, only to find her bunk empty.

I existed at Camp Auctus without really attending.

Cassie, Tori, Hannah, and Uleili tried being nice, but it was also like they were under some unspoken obligation, as if Lizzie had given them specific instructions to include me in everything they did, even though the probably hated me. Well, maybe not hated me, but she was right when she said they hardly knew me. I only had myself to blame for that. I knew that.

Since she left, nothing had been the same. I played all the games, memorized all the speeches, created all the art projects, learned all the civics lessons, listened to all the guest speakers of successful

American women, ate all the ice cream and sprinkles, and pretended to sing all the campfire songs, but I roamed the place like the Ghost of Camp Auctus Past. Not really there, not really anywhere.

Mostly, I spent time alone in the Writer's Hut. It was the best part (for me) about being away from home. I didn't know why, but Ms. Caroline kept letting me. Still, I made an effort to hang out with the cabin girls.

One night before dinner, I headed toward the mess hall at the same time they did without really interacting with any of them. I think they were shocked I was walking alongside them. I was trying to think of the next step to take, like maybe starting a conversation, to be the Julia that Lizzie, my mom, and the whole world wanted me to be, a "sociable" version of myself in an alternate reality, when Cassie caught up to me.

"Julia, you gonna sit with us this time?"

"Oh, uh…sure," I said. "If that's okay."

"Sure, fine by me." As if it wasn't fine by some of the others.

"Sorry I've been kind of absent half the time."

"You're busy writing a book. I get it. Lizzie explained." Cassie shrugged. I knew I could count on her to understand, but the other girls weren't onboard. I could tell from the looks they were always giving me.

Tori caught up to us, too. "Are you still mad?"

"What?" I was caught off guard.

"About Elizabeth leaving. Are you still mad? I mean, it's been a week."

"Like she's supposed to stop how she's feeling just because it's been a week?" Cassie scoffed. "Did you stop being mad at your brother when he told your parents you were sneaking out of the house every night to sit on the condo roof?"

"They knew I was doing that," Tori said.

"No, they didn't. I remember you cried for days when they grounded you."

Tori didn't respond. "So, are you?" she asked me again. "Still mad?"

"I'm…" Not mad, I wished I could say, but it'd be a lie.

"Don't answer that, Julia," Cassie snapped.

Naomi, Tinay's friend, showed up, stepping alongside us. She looked straight at me and said, "Finally, the author joins us." Just those words set me back to square one. Maybe because she added a giggle at the end. These girls didn't know what to make of me, and every time I tried to fit in, I was reminded just how much I didn't. And probably never would.

Without Lizzie here to defend me, the truth about their feelings would soon come out. I tried not to let Naomi's comment bother me. I wasn't a social butterfly, but I was trying. I mean, I hadn't called my mom to come get me yet. Nobody knew it, but for me, that was a real accomplishment.

Still, I didn't.

And that was, at least, something.

After the awkward dinner, I returned to the Writer's Hut to work on my book. The night was breezy, and the cicadas were loud, and anyone sitting in that little cabin could've written a book. I was shocked more people didn't love the hut. When I checked my progress, I was surprised to find I was about halfway through (fifty pages!), but how was I supposed to finish a story about friendship when my best friend had gone? Lizzie had been my muse.

After a while, somebody knocked. I jumped in my seat, not having heard footsteps coming up the walk. I guess I had been deeply into the 4th of July fireworks scene of my novel. I stood to open the door, but Ms. Caroline was already pulling the door open. "Julia, dear! The great novelist!"

I never got tired of hearing that. "Hey, Ms. C., you sure it's okay that I'm in here so much?"

She pulled off her baseball hat and ran a hand through her gray hair. "You remember what I told you. You can be here as long as we're not doing a group activity. I like to encourage you girls' individual pursuits, and I've noticed this environment has been conducive for your creativity, Julia. Sometimes that happens. Sometimes girls come here, and something about the change in environment sparks an idea. I believe in running with it. Never waste an opportunity for growth."

I nodded. I liked the way she thought, showing care and understanding.

"Although…"

Uh, oh…

"In your case, you could use growth in other areas, too. I'm sure you already know that and don't need me to tell you." She opened up a paper fan and blasted her face with air.

"Yes, I know my faults." I stared out the window at the dim lights of the lakeside lampposts, at the girls promenading up and down, taking their nightly strolls. If only I could join them, but I felt like the friendships had already been made. Too late to start a

115

new one. "Was my mom the same way?"

"Your mom?" Her face lit up, as though pleased with the opportunity to talk about something she knew and I didn't. "Julia, your mother was very much like you at this age. Talking to her now, you'd have never guessed that she was once shy, but she was, though not as painfully so as you are, dear."

I blushed.

"She and Emma had a very special bond that formed here in 2014, I believe? I still remember it like it was yesterday. I've been lucky enough to see three generations of amazing women pass through here, in some cases."

"Can you tell me about the summer they met? If you remember, that is. I know you've met a lot of campers over the years." Even though it was getting late, Ms. Caroline was in shutting-off mode and more likely to unwind with a good story.

"Will it help you write your novel?" she asked.

I nodded.

No, it wouldn't, but I needed a distraction. "Let's say yes."

"Fine. But the fast version tonight. I'll go into detail another day. Let's see, where to begin…"

She started with the part I'd heard many times before—how Emma had been coming to Camp Auctus a few years before my mother, Rebecca Miller, joined. Same as Lizzie and me. "They were different in many ways. Emma was outgoing while Rebecca was more reserved, and Emma was more likely to perform a song, while Rebecca was more likely to write it. They reminded me of the girls from that old movie, *The Parent Trap*."

I didn't know what movie she was talking about.

"Were they like twins? Because even now, they're like twins."

"Like fraternal twins, yes," she replied. "Anyone who meets them now assumes they're blood sisters. But I was lucky enough to see that bond form before my very eyes. When lifelong friendships form, it makes my work here over the years worthwhile."

I listened to Ms. Caroline a long time. She even went through the list of all my mom's camp friends— Deserae, Samantha, Lucy, Amaal. I could picture each and every one of those girls from Ms. C's descriptions. My mom was exactly as I expected her to be at my age, but looking at Ms. Caroline's face, her wrinkles, the thin skin on her hands made me feel sad all of a sudden. Time moved on, whether you liked it or not. People got old, people who were once young and perky. Talking to older people always made me feel that way.

"Those girls had something special, to be sure, Julia."

I pressed my lips into a sad smirk. "I get it. That's how Lizzie and I are."

"And it's wonderful. Life blessed you with a sister from another mister!" Ms. Caroline threw her head back and laughed. "Sorry, I love that phrase. Anyway, they did a lot that summer. We went on our White Mountains field trip. That was when one of our CITs, Jena, fell off the edge of a cliff and survived."

"What?!"

"Yes. A story for another time, but that was one of the incidents that pulled all the girls together that year. There was some discord with the Camp Infremo girls, but when it counted, they knew how to work together. I was very proud of them."

"Was that…the Council, or something? I've heard my mom talk about them."

"Yes, the Council of Friends." Ms. Caroline stretched. She was slowing down. "That's what they called their group of friends all dedicated to helping those in need. After that incident, it was election week at camp, and Cabin Infremo was like no other group of girls here. Each of them brought her strengths to the table. They learned about camaraderie, how to listen to each other; they learned the art of compromise. It was a marvelous transformation. They had their flyers, slogans…"

Man, they really went all out. I felt severely lacking in Camp Auctus tradition.

Ms. Caroline had a twinkle in her eye. "Their election jingles… Those girls were on fire. Oh, and so was the BBQ lunch they threw for the camp. Hoo-whee! That BBQ was mm-mm-good. Deserae got her parents to send up mounds of BBQ. The camp went crazy over it. I remember it like it was yesterday."

The imagery seemed to fade from Ms. Caroline's eyes, as she came back to the present.

"That sounds amazing," I said.

"Oh, it was. It was. I do believe that several of the vegetarian campers converted just for that day." She laughed. I wasn't talking about the BBQ. I was talking about the friendship, but I smiled anyway. "Anyway, it's almost time for bed. Are you about done here?"

"Yes, I'll finish up. Thanks for the story, Ms. Caroline."

"Stories are the fires that keep humanity

strong," she said, grabbing her hat and heading out the door. "Everything we do, we do so we can tell others about it one day. See you in the common area."

When Ms. Caroline left, I closed up and headed for the lake to sit on the sand.

Thinking about how deep my mom and aunt's friendship made me feel sad about my own experience at camp. I should've tried harder to make friends. I should've listened more to Lizzie. We could've had a "Council of Friends," too. Instead, I'd been stubborn. If I'd have joined in more activities, maybe we would've had more fun. Maybe she left because I'd bored her.

Tears slipped down my cheeks. I wanted them all out before I rejoined the others in the common area. Elizabeth was to me what Aunt Emma was to my mother—a sister, a forever friendship. And I'd ruined it.

FIFTEEN

Another week went by.

I was starting to turn a corner. Cassie kept talking to me more, like did I know that when she was little, she was diagnosed with Nephrotic Syndrome? It's when her kidney can't process protein right so the stuff gets deposited into the bloodstream causing a bunch of problems, which was why her mother had her on whole foods her whole life.

Also, I didn't know this either, but Tori's grandparents were from Argentina so her mother was born there, and her father came to the U.S. from Singapore when he was little, so she speaks fluent Spanish with this thick, almost-German sounding accent. Cassie and I would laugh whenever she said, "*Vámonos a la pileta imediatamente*," which meant, "Let's go to the pool immediately!"

I guess Lizzie was right, I just had to get to know them.

Thing was, it took me a long time to make friends back home, sometimes a whole school year, so summer wasn't long enough for me to come out of my shell. I still missed her, though. She was the glue that held our separate pieces together, be we could do this—we could remain friends without her.

I'd set aside my writing in order to spend more time with my cabin mates, hoping it wasn't too late to experience some of that "council of friends" bonding my mother, Aunt Emma, and their camp mates shared during their time here.

Ms. Caroline seemed pleased with my progress. Every morning, she'd give me the lowdown on where Aunt Emma was campaigning today (yesterday it was Austin, Texas). She'd show me photos of Lizzie handing out stickers, flyers, banners, or whatever swag they had that day, shaking hands with people and smiling with her mom. I could tell she was having fun. For that I was glad, but I still had to turn away from the images, saying, "That's nice," or else I'd be prone to crying again.

This morning, I hadn't seen Ms. Caroline. The counselors were handling much of the agenda without the directors' help. Maybe she'd taken a day off? But as we headed to lunch, we took the route past Ms. Caroline's office, so I could see what she was up to. I totally expected her to be outside waiting to show me the most current photos of Lizzie's whereabouts. Instead, the door was ajar and I saw Ms. Caroline inside on the phone. She faced a wall, talking and nodding, like she did whenever she was on an important call and didn't want anyone bothering her. Ms. Susan stood behind her, leaning in for a better listen.

I paused outside the door, peering in. Something was different.

"You coming?" Cassie asked.

"Yeah, go ahead. I'll catch up with you," I whispered. "Just need to speak with Ms. Caroline a second."

"We'll save you a seat." Cassie headed off to the mess hall with Tori. Behind them, Naomi bumped Tina's shoulder, as they shared a secretive giggle. I didn't know what that was about, and I didn't care anymore. I only wanted to know what was going on inside the director's office.

"Mm-hmm, mm-hmm..." Ms. Caroline listened deeply.

Ms. Susan covered her eyes, as though silently praying. Worry lines had created a road map all over her face where before there'd been nothing but smiles.

"Understood," Ms. Caroline continued in a subdued voice. "I'm so incredibly sorry for your loss."

Loss?

"Yes, I will tell her. Though I don't know how to..." She broke off. Her shoulders shook as Ms. Susan stood by holding her steady. "Oh dear, I've never had to do this."

Do what? What had Ms. Caroline never had to do before? That woman had traveled the world, seen girls come and go, year after year, directed camp, had lunch with famous congresswomen, and God knew what else. She could handle anything.

Ms. Caroline ended the call. When she turned to look at Ms. Susan, her eyes were rimmed with red, and the skin surrounding them was puffy and shiny. "What do we tell her, Sue?"

I sank bank and watched through the gap between the door, the hinges, and the frame.

"The truth," Ms. Susan said. "She was shot at the election rally and died on the way to the hospital." Ms. Susan pressed her lips together, opened her arms, and Ms. Caroline, helpless and weak. shrank into them, sobbing quietly against petite Ms. Susan's shoulder.

Wait, who...?

Who was shot?

Election rally?

My stomach leaped and did a clunky roll, colliding with my ribcage. I felt unsteady and held onto the door frame. I only knew two people at an election rally and loved both of them.

Then, I heard it... "My God, she was only a child."

I gasped. Slapped my hand over my mouth. It was too late to hide my surprise. Both Ms. Caroline and Ms. Susan had heard me in the doorway and whipped their faces to the spot where I stood rooted to the ground, unable to move.

"Damn it..." Ms. Caroline stared at me.

In just one look, I felt time slow down and knew everything was about to change.

She gave Ms. Susan a look like maybe they should've closed the door before taking the call. "Oh, honey, I'm so sorry." Ms. Caroline flew across the office in my direction, but all I heard were the words she'd uttered.

The election rally...she was only a child...shot and died.

Suddenly, I felt dizzy, as the pungent smell of humid earth and overnight rain overwhelmed me. I held onto the door, as Ms. Caroline and Ms. Susan formed a net of adult hands and arms around my shoulders to keep me from falling too fast. I began losing consciousness, sliding downward, down a black tunnel until my face rested on the ground, same as it had the day of the races.

The election rally...

...she was only a child...

...shot and died.

I imagined Lizzie lying on the floor in a pool of her own blood. They couldn't have meant Lizzie, could they? I was aware of more people around me, girls of all ages asking if I was okay. And finally, I blacked out completely.

Lying for what seemed like forever with cool towels pressed to my forehead, I tried to piece together the events. I'd heard girls chatting nervously, the adults scrambling to find help, Ms. Caroline ordering everyone to carry on as usual while she and the other team members figured this out. My eyes opened slowly to see the ceiling of her office. There was dust up there that'd probably been there a very long time.

Why was I here again?

Outside the window, I heard two girls talking about it. "Elizabeth Richards...you know, the senator's daughter. Yeah, her..." And I sat up quickly.

"What happened, Ms. Caroline? Why am I here?"

"Honey, Nurse Annelle put you there because you weren't feeling well. Do you...do you not remember anything you heard?"

"I remember...." And suddenly, the memory hit me. I'd hoped I'd been dreaming, but it was real. I was pretty sure, from the hubbub outside, and the girls trying to get a peek of me through the window, that something bad had happened. "Is Lizzie okay?"

"No, honey." Her eyes filled with tears. "Lizzie is not okay. I'm sorry to tell you that…she's gone, sweetheart. They tried to save her, but…they couldn't."

"She's dead?" I knew it was a stupid question, but I just needed it confirmed. "Is that what you're telling me?"

The tears spilled over her eyelids, as she nodded and choked on her own words. "Yes," she squeaked. "There was a shooter at the rally. Lizzie and eleven others were amongst the victims."

"And my aunt?"

"Your aunt is alive, though this will certainly kill her, I'm sure." She broke into tears again then thought better of it and swallowed them back up, as if for my sake. "I don't understand this world. I just don't. What do I do, oh Lord? What do I do?" She was no longer talking to me and instead asking for guidance. It was disheartening to see her praying like this. I knew that it was bad.

I couldn't feel a thing. This wasn't happening. She was fine yesterday. I saw a photo of her on Ms. Caroline's phone, smiling and shaking hands with some old guy. This was certainly a misunderstanding of some kind. There was no way my lively, happy golden girl was dead.

It was impossible.

"I'm sorry, I…" Ms. Caroline couldn't speak anymore and tapped Ms. Susan on the shoulder.

Ms. Susan nodded, wiped tears from her eyes, then slapped on a kind smile. "Julia, honey, why don't we go get you something to eat? You'll feel better when you have something in your stomach." Clearly, she was helping Ms. Caroline do her job, because Ms. Caroline was in shock.

But I couldn't eat. The idea that Elizabeth would never have food in her stomach again made me even sicker, and I lay down underneath the window sill again. For the next hour, I didn't cry, didn't move, didn't even blink. All I could do was envision her at the rally, where she'd stood, how it had happened. Did she try to run? Did she turn, blond hair whipping around her, ready to greet someone new like she loved to do and find herself face-to-face with the barrel of a gun?

"Come on, honey. Just a bite," Ms. Caroline was back with a plate of pasta salad.

No.

I wasn't there anymore. I'd lifted out of my body and traveled across the miles to Texas. Where was my cousin now? Was she at the hospital, dead with doctors all around her? Was she lying in a bed or had someone slid her into a cold, metal drawer like I'd seen in a movie once?

I must've said yes to something Ms. Susan said, because I let her guide me down the hallway out into the cloudy world of rural Massachusetts and through Ms. Caroline's grassy garden. Just a week ago, Elizabeth had stood in that spot right there, alive and hugging me. Maybe if I'd begged her to stay. If I'd fought harder. Been madder at her, *made* her feel guilty, *made* her stay, she would be alive right now.

But I hadn't. I'd let her go. I'd tried being happy for her, and now look.

This was my fault.

She was dead because of me.

We came to the door of the mess hall and paused just outside. Normally, the noises from inside leaked out of the room. Girls chattering about school, boys, movies, celebrities, and their plans for the last days of summer: Europe, cruises to Alaska, fancy bat mitzvahs, and quinceañeras.

None of that now.

Only the quiet tones of Ms. Caroline addressing the girls. "I'm taking her to the airport, so I'll be back late tonight..." The microphone squawked.

Ms. Susan looked at me curiously, then pulled on the door just a bit. "Wait a minute here." She poked her head in.

"We need to be strong, hold it together..." Ms. Caroline was saying. "It's okay to feel sad and angry. But these things happen very rarely, so you don't need to be afraid."

Silence across the mess hall.

More feedback from the microphone.

I may not have been able to hear everything Ms. Caroline was saying, but I'd always remember that screechy metallic sound and this moment. Ms. Susan came back and closed the door softly. "We should go back. I'll bring you the ice cream myself. How does that sound?"

How does that sound? That sounded alien. Confusing. How could ice cream even exist without Lizzie? I'd only ever known a world with her in it. How was I supposed to enjoy it now? How was I supposed to even live in a world where she didn't exist?

I could hear Ms. Caroline, "I ask for a moment of silence for our fellow camper, Elizabeth. If you pray, please say a prayer for her mother..." Even from outside I heard somebody crying. "…her grandparents, and our fellow camper Julia and her parents."

Me.

Ms. Susan urged me away from the mess hall. Quietly we walked back to the director's office in light drizzling rain and faraway thunder. The most disturbing part was how I couldn't feel a thing. For two weeks, I'd dealt with sad feelings that she was gone, when really she'd been in the world, just apart from me. And now that she was really, truly gone from the world, I couldn't feel the sadness everyone seemed to be feeling.

I felt.

Absolutely.

Nothing.

SIXTEEN

I stared out the window at fluffy orange clouds streaked with the last light of day.

If all Pastor Bryan from my aunt's church had ever said was true, those we loved who'd passed on were up in Heaven, higher than those clouds. That meant my mom and I were closer to Lizzie right now, up in this plane. But that gave me little consolation. I didn't want her in Heaven with God—I wanted her here.

On Earth.

With me.

Where she belonged.

The more I thought about it, the more this had to be a mistake, a bad dream, from the moment I'd woken up. Even though I'd learned about Lizzie just this morning, it still hadn't hit home. It wasn't possible. She was still on the campaign tour with her mom, shaking hands with people and smiling for photos, while I was going home to Boca with my mom. That's all. Nothing else.

I'd still see her in a few weeks when we'd do our video series together. Ms. Caroline must've been given the wrong information, because there was no way that my Elizabeth, the girl that shone with an inner light, was now lifeless.

But the cues around me said otherwise. Why else would the airline steward keep asking us if we needed anything with that sympathetic head tilt? Why else could I hear others in the rows behind him talking about "the shooting," "the tragedy?" Why would my mother be sobbing into the backrest of the seat? Why else would she continually shake her head and quietly pray to God, "This can't be. Why have you done this?" Why would she then shake from the inside of her soul, grip my hand, and contort her face with all the agony she was trying so hard to hold in?

I let her grip my hand, but I kept turning to the window and staring out at those clouds.

God, I don't understand what's happening. With so many bad people in the world, why would you take my cousin? Lizzie only tried to do good things. It doesn't make sense. That's why this can't be real.

Perhaps if I closed my eyes and prayed for it all to go away, it would. When I reopened them, we'd be landing in Florida, and all would be back to the way it was. My mother would be asking a million questions about camp, telling me stories about the past, and I'd be annoyed by her questions, but at least it'd all be normal.

Mom controlled her sob. "They're bringing her home the day after tomorrow."

What did that mean "bringing her home?" Did that mean they would actually send a dead body to Florida? I thought when a person died, they stayed where they were, which would be Houston, in this case.

"The funeral will be Thursday," she sniffed. "Would you like to say something?"

"What do you mean?"

"To the people who come? You knew her best. You should probably say a few words?"

A few words? Did my mother know me at all? I couldn't even say a few words in the best of circumstances, when life was happy, but she was asking if I could say a few words in front of a hundred people or more for the funeral of my dearest cousin?

"I can't."

And that made me feel guilty beyond belief. I was able to come up with thousands of words about our friendship for a book I was writing, a book I had to leave behind that Ms. Caroline said she would send me, but I couldn't say important words when it mattered?

"It doesn't have to be memorized. You could write it down then read it," she said in the soft, assuring voice she used whenever she wanted to convince me to do something.

I said nothing.

"What are you thinking right now, baby?"

Little did she know her daughter, Julia, wasn't home right now. It may have looked like me, but inside, I had no idea what to think or feel. The lights were off in my head and would stay dark for a long, long time.

She patted my hand. "I understand. Whatever you're feeling is okay."

If that was true, then empty was how I felt—and it didn't feel okay.

We arrived at Ft. Lauderdale Airport, and my mom's phone immediately began blowing up with messages from concerned people who'd heard the news. We made our way off the plane, as the stewards and pilots stood at the entrance, shaking our hands. "Our deepest condolences," they all said, bowing their heads.

Was that it? Was that the most people could do when somebody died, was utter a few meaningless words? There had to be a way to actually fix this, something that could be said or done to actually reverse or change the outcome. Words and a handshake did nothing. If Lizzie were here, she'd do more.

My mother thanked them kindly anyway, as we disembarked, and I gave them sour looks as I stepped into the tunnel, clinging to her side. One of the airline workers carried our bags for us, and when we stepped into the terminal, more employees there told us how sorry they were for our loss.

"I hope they catch the guy," one lady said. "I'm going to pray that they do."

"Thank you," my mother said awkwardly. She must've thought it was an odd thing to tell a person, same as I did.

"If there's anything you need…" Another man from the airline followed us a few more steps until we were out of the gate.

My mother thanked him and the group of employees watching us leave, which was more attention than we'd received so far, and we were somewhat used to being treated specially by people we didn't know, people who knew our connection to my aunt, the senator. As we walked through the terminal, screens up near the ceiling broadcasted the news about the Election Rally Shooting, they were calling it. I heard snippets of things the reporters said, which changed depending on which screen we passed.

"...not releasing the names of the eleven victims until all family members are notified..."

"...one of them a child of twelve years of age..."

How had the airline people known it was related to us then? Good news traveled fast.

My mother then stopped and gawked at another screen, pressing a tissue to her nose. *Shooter Found Dead Inside Home,* the headline said. My mother bit her bottom lip, and her eyes welled up again, and I thought that was odd because if I felt anything at all, it was happy that the person responsible for this would no longer be able to hurt anyone else.

"Let's go." She pulled me along. "Your father is waiting for us."

We followed all the signs for baggage claim and paused for breath when we reached the carousel. When I finally saw my father, the sad smile on his face and his open arms, something inside of me woke up. I ran over to him for a hug and pressed my face into his chest.

"Hey, pumpkin," he said, kissing my hair. He hugged me harder than I'd ever felt before, as if he might lose me if he let me go. I could even feel him shaking a little bit on the inside.

"Hi, Dad." I loved the smell of his shirt, the solidness of my father's arms.

My mother wrapped her arms around us both, and for a few seconds, I felt safe again. Inside, I felt like Jell-O being wiggled around, but on the outside, I had to act strong. Something told me if I didn't, I would lose control. "She hasn't eaten," my mother said.

It was true, but I couldn't eat even if I wanted to. The thought of food all day had made my stomach turn over and over again. My parents pulled back and began talking in hushed tones and code, as other passengers began pooling around the carousel, and the truth about this horrible day began settling around me once again.

Near the carousel bend, two men stood talking, one young, one older. They were happy to see each other too, except they were loud, talking about the trip the younger one had taken, and maybe they didn't realize it, but I could hear what they were saying. My parents didn't because they were disengaged from any conversations besides their own, but I suddenly felt psychic, as though I could hear the voices of everyone around me.

"I know, can you believe it?" the older one said, shaking his head.

"Too bad he didn't take her out along with the rest," the young man laughed then quietly, thinking nobody could hear him, muttered, "Dumb bitch."

But I did. I heard him.

Take out whom? I focused my hearing as hard as I could.

"Would've made this election a lot easier if he had," the other one mumbled. Both looked around to see if anyone was listening, but neither saw me watching closely, reading lips.

My stomach hardened into the tightest of knots.

"Maybe this'll finally put pressure on her to drop out."

"Yeah, she'll drop out. With her kid dead? I'm sure of it."

It was the laughter.

The laughter between the two men, like this might've been a good thing to happen. The laughter and the way they brushed off the topic, moved onto something else in their conversation, work, money, and the weather, that dislodged something inside of me. Deep within my chest, a lock twisted and broke off. A gate creaked open. A feeling I did not recognize rose up and washed over me, as I listened to the two men casually chat about my aunt and cousin like they weren't worth another minute. Like there were better things to discuss.

Her dead kid.

They were talking about Lizzie. My best friend, my sister, the girl I knew and loved like nobody else in this awful world. Two strangers discussing how good it was that she was now dead. How great that would be for the election. So freakin hilarious.

I pried myself away from my dad and, before I could think about what I was doing, charged at the younger, thinner of the two men. I wasn't sure why him, probably because his face looked the most smug. My body rammed into him with everything I had in me. My soul wanted nothing but to knock the fool down, my fists pummeling into his stomach and side. I was sure it felt like nothing to him being three times my size, which only made me hit even harder.

Voices shouted. The older man grabbed my shoulders and cried to get this girl off his son. Other voices crowded around us. My father worked to disentangle my left arm from around the man's back. The man himself shoved his fist into my lower back to get me to let go, and that was when the blur came.

135

Without knowing how it happened, I landed on the floor, but my father had taken my place, punching the man hard in the face before pushing him against a column, as my mother helplessly flailed her arms and shouted. All I could do was watch, loving my father for fighting on my behalf without even knowing what had prompted me to attack.

He didn't know, and he didn't care. All he cared was that this man had put his hands on me.

"How dare you hit a child..." My mother was screaming. "How dare you? You should be ashamed of yourself!"

But it wasn't the jab at my back that had hurt anywhere near the strangers' callousness, their not-caring about the victims at the rally shooting. How could they not? How could the deaths of innocent people be a good thing?

"You're what's wrong with this country," my father grunted, shoving a finger in the man's face, as security officers arrived, and all the adults started exchanging accounts of what happened.

I sat on the floor shaking, my mother cross-legged next to me, arms around me. "Jules? It's okay, honey." Apparently, the reason why I'd lashed out didn't matter, and inside I felt a horrible gnawing, dawning realization I couldn't name.

Two women nearby reported on what they heard. They told my parents how they'd overheard the same abominable conversation I'd had. One of them looked at me. "Good on you, little girl. I would've done the same."

Until that moment, I'd never imagined that anyone would not care about a child dying. We believe we're special, that the loss of a young person, of any good person, is sad and a tragedy for all, but in these men's voices, I heard the truth—not everyone in this world cares about children or lives for that matter. To people who didn't care, today's tragedy had been a joke, and I finally knew the emotion I felt.

Grief.

SEVENTEEN

The dress was mossy green with white swirls in the pattern and no shape in the waist. It made me look like an old lady in temple, especially with the white shoes my mother picked out, but I wore the ensemble anyway. I didn't want to fight with Mom about her picking clothes out for me. Then again, she was so distraught, she probably wouldn't have noticed if I changed into another dress anyway.

Lizzie would've laughed at it. She would've told me I looked like seaweed.

I decided to keep it on. The idea of Lizzie laughing at the dress I wore to her funeral was the only thing that would get me through this day. Besides, I felt like seaweed, getting tossed and pushed around by ocean waves too strong for me to battle, so it felt appropriate.

In the hallway, my father announced we'd be leaving in ten minutes. I finished ironing my hair and putting on lip gloss, hair and makeup being two of the only things I could control today. I picked up my phone without thinking and began a message to Lizzie to ask how she was doing her hair for the funeral, so we could match, when I realized the sheer truth of that stupidity.

I put the phone down, swallowed a ball forming in my throat. Finality hit me like a flying brick. Lizzie would never reply to any of my messages ever again.

I stared into the bathroom mirror at the girl standing there. My face lacked color even though I'd spent half the summer outdoors, and my eyes looked tired. I thought of all the photos I'd taken over the years with Lizzie, the two of us with arms around each other, smiling goofily or sticking out our tongues. She wouldn't be in any of today's photos. And she wouldn't be telling me what clothes she was wearing or how she was doing her hair ever again.

I had no one to match with.

On the way to the wake, my father did his best to prepare me for what was coming. After several exchanged glances with my mother, he looked in the rearview mirror. "Julia, you should know that the funeral will be open casket."

Silence. I shifted my focus to the trees outside, the sparkling canals, and the palm trees sprouting high into the sky.

"Open casket means that you will be able to see Lizzie's body inside the casket."

More silence. I figured what open casket meant just from the context clues, but I let Dad do his thing. After the way he beat the crap out of that guy at the airport after he "laid his hand on me," my dad could say anything he wanted.

Dad's hands gripped the steering wheel. "Your mother and I want you to know that you don't have to come up to the casket if you don't want to, pumpkin.

You can be as close or as far as you want. Whatever you feel is right."

Mom's face was turned toward the window. I could see her fist up to her mouth which meant she was crying again, or biting down the tears so I wouldn't see her.

"Julia?" His eyes searched for mine in the rearview mirror.

I met his gaze. "I heard you, Dad."

"Okay, just want to make sure you understand. There's no wrong or right way to behave at the funeral. If you want to stay away, we can understand that," Dad said, almost as though he and Mom wished I would— stay away, that was.

I thought about what I would see when we walked into the funeral home. I'd never been to a funeral before and had no idea what to expect, and I didn't want to ask my parents questions and risk sounding stupid. Would she be in the middle of the room and everyone walk around it? Would she look like Snow White, sleeping in the glass case? Would we all see the bullet holes where she was shot? Maybe we wouldn't be allowed to touch her, or maybe there'd be ropes surrounding her like the mummies in the museum we'd visited in Egypt last year.

Dad said there was no wrong or right way to behave. What if I wanted to sit in the car and refuse to go inside? Would that be cool?

When we arrived and Dad pulled into the parking lot, I could already see the somber faces of the adults parading into the building and knew this wasn't going to be good. "I don't want to talk to anyone," I said suddenly.

Mom twisted her head to me, as she grabbed the sign-in book she'd made for Aunt Emma. "What's that, honey?"

"I said, I don't want to talk to anyone. I know that people are going to say things to me, and I don't want to talk back. It's just going to be fake, whatever I say."

Mom looked at Dad for support, their silent "united front" means of communication. Dad was already halfway out of the car and opened my side door. "That's fine, Julia. You don't have to talk to anyone. Most people won't expect you to say anything back anyway. They only want to pay their respects to you."

Every step out of the car and toward the funeral parlor reminded me of the field trip we took to the Everglades two years ago when we all walked through the murky water up to our waists. Felt like we were wading through honey mixed with molasses, working so hard just to take two steps.

We finally made it into the building. The first thing I noticed were the huge floral arrangements on either side of a big, framed photo of Lizzie in sixth grade. She hated that picture of herself and even threatened to draw mustache and beard on it with a marker if her mother didn't take it down from the foyer entrance, yet there it was.

Sorry, Lizzie, I thought. *If I'd known your mom was going to put that up, I would've fought for you.* It made me think about my own funeral. If I died at a young age, would my mom put all the photos of myself that I hated up for everyone to look at? The lack of

choice and control over this life in the last three days
had been staggering.

Even though we were five minutes early, there
were fifty people inside already. Immediately,
Granddad and Grandma Wendy came up to us, hugging
each of us for a really long time in silence. Dad was
right—nobody expected me to say anything. An
unspoken truth about funerals—there are no words.
Grandma Wendy put her arm around me as if to protect
me from sharks in the water, to steer me like a boat
wherever she wanted me to go, which I quickly learned
was away from the casket.

I saw it from across the room. It was a long,
silver box with half its lid open. The inside lining of the
lid was a shiny satin gray, and someone had pinned
photos to the lining. I couldn't see what was in the
photos, but they were probably pictures of her. I
gravitated toward a seat near the back with Grandma
Wendy who led us there and patted my hand the whole
time we were sitting. From this distance, all I could see
of Lizzie were her hands. Her pale fingers folded and
resting on top of her stomach, holding something in
them.

"Do you want to move closer?" she asked.
I nodded.
Grandma Wendy stood, smiled at a few people
who looked like they wanted to say hello to me, and
quickly maneuvered me into a closer row. Always
patting my hand protectively, always nodding at the
strangers who'd approach hesitantly. The message was
clear—my granddaughter doesn't want to talk right
now.

As the funeral parlor filled with what had to easily be two or three hundred people, my grandmother inched me closer to the front. Each time we moved seats, I could see a little bit more of Lizzie. *Lizzie's body*, I kept telling myself. The real Lizzie was, at this moment, riding over some rainbow on a white horse, giggling at the fuss all these adults were making over her.

My heart beat wildly inside my chest on the last move. I could see the white dress she wore and golden tresses laid over her shoulders in long waves. In her hands she held Clark, the little brown teddy bear she'd had all her life since she was a baby. I swallowed hard. This would be the last time I'd see her hold that bear.

We finally moved to the second row right behind Aunt Emma who sat straight in front of the casket, into two saved seats next to my parents and Grandpa. Aunt Emma's shoulders shook uncontrollably, her head hung low, as my mother caressed her hair off her back and whispered in her ear, as person after person lined up to say something to her. Aunt Emma was nice enough to nod and smile to each person who talked to her. I wouldn't have wanted anyone near me.

During a break in the condolences, I heard Aunt Emma crying to my mom. She kept saying, "This is my fault, this is my fault. If I hadn't taken her with me, we wouldn't be here. She'd still be with me."

My mom and uncle hushed her, rubbed her back and did everything they could to convince Aunt Emma that no—it'd been a tragedy, a mistake—there was nothing she could've done to prevent it. It was simply Lizzie's time to go. God had "called her home." But that made me mad inside. It hadn't been Lizzie's time to go. I wholeheartedly agreed with Aunt Emma. She shouldn't have taken Lizzie on her election rally tour. Lizzie was supposed to stay at Camp Auctus where she'd have been safe.

With me.

I would never tell Aunt Emma that, though. I'd eat my words and swallow my anger for the rest of my life, because I didn't see the point. Lizzie was already dead. Telling her that wouldn't bring her back to life. But Lizzie had been cut from the same cloth as Aunt Emma—adventurous, outgoing, not afraid of anything in this world.

I wished she'd been just a little bit afraid. Just a little. She might still be here.

Pastor Bryan arrived. He said some nice things about Lizzie, but nothing that really brought out the real person we all knew. He could've been talking about anyone, but he talked a lot about finding peace during times like this and mentioned how God had a plan. What could God's plan have possibly been to have a child shot in the back? I didn't know the details of Lizzie's death, but I kept imagining her lying on her stomach, shot in the back.

I shook my head to clear the image. How was any of this possible? Even now, staring at her profile in the silver box, I couldn't believe it was truly her lying there. My mother finally stood after the sermon and mustered up the courage to walk forward and kneel on the little step. My father glanced back at me, to see how I was doing, or to see how I'd react. I kept my eyes down.

Could I go up and do the same? Could I see her up close?

"You know, when Emma's father passed away…" Grandma Wendy squeezed my hand, as she looked straight ahead. "I almost didn't see him in the casket," she said. At first, I was confused then remembered that her first husband, Aunt Emma's actual dad, had died in the attack on the World Trade Center on 9/11.

I looked at her.

She smiled softly and squeezed my hand. "But I'm glad I did. I would've spent the rest of my life wishing I could've said goodbye." I knew what she was telling me. And even though my father told me it was my choice, I had to admit I agreed with Grandma. If I didn't say goodbye to her face right now, I'd never get another chance.

Suddenly, I stood, feeling the eyes of hundreds of guests on me.

I walked over to the casket.

EIGHTEEN

Forget Snow White in the glass case. Lizzie looked like Sleeping Beauty. With her blonde hair cascading over her shoulders, she looked like a beautiful, resting angel in a white gauzy dress. She looked innocent, like the child she was, younger than her twelve years of age, like some Renaissance artist had painted her and named her *The Floating Girl.*

I wanted to cry like other people had, but my gaze was transfixed on her timeless beauty. Had she looked lifeless, it would've made it easier to accept that she was dead, but to me, it seemed like she would awaken at any second. Her cheeks were pink but not from the inside, more like dusty blush had made her that way. Her mouth was turned into the slightest of smiles, as if there were something amusing about all this.

On either side of me, my mom and Aunt Emma appeared, resting their arms around me. I lay my hand on top of Lizzie's holding Clark, the teddy bear, expecting to feel warm, supple skin, but she was cold and dry. The "body" was. Like the real Lizzie had left and all that remained was this empty wax vessel.

So this was death.

I pulled my hand back, kept it perched on the edge of the casket.

She was gone, for sure. This wasn't some dream or nightmare. This was real.

I inhaled a deep breath to keep the ball in my stomach from imploding, to keep my energy center from fizzling out and never caring again. What could I tell Lizzie now that I was here, sharing the same space with her, my special few minutes apart from the other guests?

"I'm sorry for what happened to you," I whispered. Aloud, the words sounded ridiculous, like she wasn't around to hear them anyway. I kept telling myself she was here—somewhere. *Just keep talking.* "It wasn't fair. You should still be with us right now."

I felt Mom and Aunt Emma's shivering, sobbing bodies without even having to look at them. And me in the middle holding them up. All I could do for the longest time was stare at my cousin's body. I never noticed how skinny her arms were until now. Then I noticed something else.

She had on a cross on a gold chain instead, something I'd never seen her wear before. "Her heart," I said, eyeing her neck.

Aunt Emma and Mom crouched to hear me better. "What was that, baby?" Mom asked.

"The heart I made for her. In summer camp. This one," I said, tugging out the ST ENDS tucked inside my seaweed dress. "She doesn't have it on."

"I don't know which heart she means," Aunt Emma murmured. "I can't remember. Which one was it, honey?" Aunt Emma had enough to deal with without me making a fuss about a missing crappy Arts & Crafts project.

"Don't worry." Maybe Lizzie had taken it off once she was on the road. Maybe she hadn't liked it or refused to wear it. Now I felt silly for wearing mine. I tucked it back inside my dress.

"Father Bryan is going to lead the prayer now." Mom tapped my shoulder. "We need to go sit."

I didn't want to sit, or stand, or stay, nor leave. I wanted to crawl up into a ball and die so I could be with Lizzie again. "I'll do the video series by myself," I whispered. "And I'll try not to be so shy, because I know you hate that. I'll try to go on without you, Lizzie, but I don't know how. You're my best—my only—friend."

Maybe if I stayed a second longer, her eyelids would flutter, we'd all see those baby blues again, she'd smile, and this day could fly into oblivion for all I cared. But she remained still. *The floating girl...*

The next morning, we were back in the same salon again, this time to close up her casket for the final time before following each other in a row of cars all the way to the cemetery. Lizzie looked exactly the same as yesterday, only reinforcing the idea that she wasn't alive anymore. She was an unplugged doll inside her pretty box.

The family stood around the casket as the funeral parlor worker stood holding the lid while waiting for everyone to see Lizzie for the last time. Aunt Emma's arms and body were draped like a flag over her daughter, and she shook so hard with grief, my heart opened up to absorb her pain. Lizzie might've been my cousin, but she was Aunt Emma's little baby girl, and somehow that was infinitely worse.

My mom looked tired from crying. I wondered if she felt grateful to have her own daughter still with her, if she felt guilty about that. After all, she'd said no to me going to the rally, wanting me to stay at camp. Had I gone, this funeral might've been for me too.

My uncle had to pull Aunt Emma away from the casket in order for the funeral man, who looked like he was used to dealing with people in tears, to do his job. When they finally closed the lid on Lizzie's face forever, I caught the last glimpse of her beautiful face. Last view of her cheeks, her upturned nose, her lips, those soft eyebrows.

Goodbye, silly girl.

The lid shut completely, as Aunt Emma fell apart against my uncle's shoulder, while I turned into my dad's suit, wishing this nightmare would finally end. Then I thought how that wasn't the last time I'd see her face. Not really. The last time I'd seen her face had been in Ms. Caroline's garden on the morning she left, when she ran off happy to be joining her mother for a new adventure.

When she left me behind. Left me in the safety of strangers.

While she went off to war.

A month later, I hadn't started the video series yet. Or rather, I did record one, but it came out so boring, I ended up deleting the whole dreadful thing. Nobody was going to watch the shiest, quietest girl in the world talk about random topics. Lizzie, on the other hand, had been born for it. I would screw this up in a huge way.

It was just as well because school started, which gave me an excuse to think about something different. I'd never been one of those school nerds who were thirsty for classes to begin, but I couldn't wait to hear about something other than the shooting. All the news stations could talk about was whether or not Senator Singletary-Richards would drop out of the presidential race, whether she would power on in her daughter's name, or whether she was too grief-stricken to go on. *The dead. The victims. The youngest of them being Senator Singletary-Richards' daughter...*

The media reminded me too much of those two men at the airport and how the death of eleven people last month during a peaceful rally had just been a source of entertainment to them. Words and ideas for people to argue about, while nobody did anything concrete to fix the problem.

That's because nobody cared about Lizzie anymore. Nobody cared about the people trying to be heard either, the people who screamed and fought on behalf of the children. Eventually, the incident slipped into the past, replaced with new things to talk about.

But I was still here, the girl who'd lost her cousin. The empty girl.

Adventures of Floating Girl and Empty Girl...

I heard from Cassie and Tori, but couldn't open up to them. Without Lizzie, they were nothing but strangers from camp, the girls who were friends with my cousin but not really with me. I treated them nice anyway, because my mother told me I should, all because they'd sent me cards, letters, and photos from the girls at Camp Auctus during their last week. Letters that said things like, "I'm sorry for your loss," from the older campers to stuff like, "I'm sorry your cousin died," from the little girls.

Now it was September and the summer felt like a distant dream. I tried keeping myself busy with Algebra, World History, Art, Science, and homework, but I always felt like something was brewing just underneath my surface. I couldn't figure out what it was. It was like being lost in my own homeland, drifting in and out of each day without purpose. Smiles weren't real and conversations even less.

In the halls, kids would look at me then glance away. Sometimes they'd whisper things to each other. *That's her. That's Elizabeth Richards' cousin.* I didn't have to hear their voices to know that was what they were saying. Teachers were extra nice. There was nothing wrong with that. But all of it was attention, whether it was directed at me or not, it was there. Reminders around every corner, when all I wanted to do was forget.

The only thing I remotely cared about in those weeks was the discussion in the news about upcoming plans to colonize Mars. Our country was in the preliminary stages of putting together teams of scientists to send to the red planet, and something about that greatly appealed to me. How amazing would it be to get away from Earth, from all the hate, violence, and senseless slaughter and go live on a lonely, isolated planet? That sounded like a dream come true, but I was only twelve, still years away from ever being ready.

However, if they needed teens for the first colonization mission, I would be there like a bear. I started decorating my room with images of Mars, articles from scientific journals, and I'd read everything I could get my hands on to do with Mars colonization. I cared about little else between September and December of 2039.

My parents tried their best to maintain a stable environment for me, but my dad had started working later than before, and I had the weird feeling he was trying to avoid my mom who wasn't handling the tragedy very well. That left me as the only person she had to talk to until Dad got home, and most of the time I didn't want to discuss anything related to "the tragedy."

There was no way to fix it. Lizzie was dead. And it'd happened because some crazy rando was able to walk in and just shoot whoever he wanted. Anybody could buy a gun. A gun for you. A gun for me. Guns for everyone! Yee-haw!

How about the adults in this world get their crap together and come up with a solution?

Every day, the knot inside my stomach grew tighter. Eating made me feel worse. My parents didn't know it, but I was ditching breakfast, skipping lunch at school, and locking myself in the bathroom after dinner to get rid of whatever was in my stomach. Sounds crazy, but it made me feel better even though I knew it was wrong. Controlling my food intake made me feel like I was at least in charge of something.

One night, I was reading an article about aerogel, the Styrofoam-like building material for Mars which had developed quite a bit in the last twenty years, when a message popped up on my social media page. It was from someone named YuGiOhCrap14 and I wasn't sure I wanted to accept it.

Hi Julia.

I was at the same rally your cousin was at.

I know how tired you are of hearing this, but I'm sorry for your loss. I mean that. If you ever want to talk about it, you can talk to me because I get it. As for your cousin?

I watched the cursor blink on the computer screen. Should I answer? I wasn't sure I wanted to commiserate with anyone about Lizzie now that I was just starting to block out the pain, not even someone who understood.

Your cousin saved my life.

NINETEEN

Staring at the words, I held my breath.

Did I want to reply and get sucked into that awful day again? I wasn't sure I wanted to relive the details I'd been given. I just wanted to keep reading about aerogel, imagining myself living out the rest of my years on Mars, far, far away from this horrible place. But I had to know what he or she meant by my cousin saved his/her/their life, or my brain would never forget it.

What do you mean

I took the bait, accepting the message. Plus, I had to know how old this person was that I chatting with, or else my father would lose his mind.

How old are you? Pronouns?

The reply came immediately. They were obviously waiting for me to respond on the other side of the digital screen.

16—he/him, sorry I should've said that.

Okay, fine, assuming he was telling the truth. He continued:

I was helping my parents who were working at your aunt's rally. I was in charge of making sure everybody had a button. Your cousin and I were both working the same area. She was in charge of handing necklaces with your aunt's slogan, "The Future is HERe" on them.

Senator Singletary-Richards had just taken the stage. People were cheering like crazy. I'd never been to a rally before, but my parents insisted I should volunteer, so I could see what went into the process. Lizzie was cheering for her mom. You should've seen her. I thought she was pretty cute the way she jumped up and down, totally fangirling. When the shots started, I thought balloons were popping. They had those big balloon arcs everywhere. But we know it wasn't balloons.

I closed my eyes and saw the scene perfectly in my mind. I had to remind myself to breathe normally. When I opened them again, the boy had written another bubble…

I turned to see lots of the audience running off to either side and that's when I saw what was causing the panic. We won't say his name. HIM. But there he was, wearing his mask and backpack, aiming that rifle right at me.

His words trailed off, as I waited with bated breath, my heart booming inside my ribcage. *And then?* I typed.

155

I've played first-person shooter games a million times. I'm sure you have too. Or any other kid my age. Believe it or not those games help me develop instincts. I flinched, because if I was playing a game, I'd flinch, or drop, or jump to the side if I saw a guy with a rifle standing there taking aim. But there was a woman standing frozen next to me and I didn't want to push the other way, because your cousin was there.

That's when I felt her push up behind me.

At first I thought she was trying to hide behind me so I spread my arms to shield her. But then she pushed me. Like HARD. I fell onto the floor onto my stomach behind a big potted plant. She landed on my foot, and that's when I started to pull at her feet, to drag her toward me. But then I saw it was too late. He'd gotten her.

I stared at the onslaught of bubbled messages. I hadn't wanted the details, but there they were. The balloons, the plant, the cheering. I could see it very clearly. In a way, I was grateful for them. For months, I'd had this image in my head of how it all went down, an image I knew was probably wrong of Lizzie running and getting hit and dropping. This helped me fill in some missing puzzle pieces.

Are you okay?

he asked.

No.

He replied:

I'm sorry I'm telling you this. But I wanted you to know that Lizzie Richards was my hero. Never screamed. Never panicked. She just pushed me, no SHOVED me out of the way. She LITERALLY SAVED me, he repeated, as if to drive the point home, then took the bullet herself.

God, I thought. I imagined her at the rally, as tears filled my eyes, methodically pushing this teen kid out of the way, as if she'd always known what to do, how to react. Lizzie had always been a leader, a thinker who knew just what to do in any situation. I'd seen it firsthand this summer at camp, which already felt like a million years ago. Whether she'd pushed the boy because she was fleeing or saving him didn't matter. This boy was here because of Lizzie.

Wow...I don't know what to say.

For months, the tears refused to come. Me, the crybaby, had not been able to muster up very many for the girl I'd loved—*still* loved—so much, all because it hadn't seemed real. Watching the recaps on the news was like watching a reality show. Most of the time, I felt like Lizzie was just off in the world somewhere, like that body I saw at the funeral had just been a stand-in for a girl who'd come home one day. But now I couldn't stop the tears from spilling over, literally dripping down my face and onto my desk.

They don't tell that part on the news, so I didn't know if you knew. Well, now you do.

I thanked him and logged off. I wasn't sure how he'd even found me, though it wasn't too difficult, once you connected the social media dots. I needed to breathe. My cousin had saved a life, just as she'd given up her own. And just like that, my life was upended again.

It took all day to process.

I didn't sleep that night, and I definitely didn't eat. In fact, food was quickly becoming a distant memory. No matter what I put in my mouth, I imagined Lizzie unable to do the same and before I knew it, my body was rejecting it. My clothes fit looser than ever before, and it was only a matter of time before my parents noticed. Already, my dad had mentioned how skinnier my face looked, so I made it a point to go downstairs to the kitchen and pretend like I was getting a snack.

Little did they know I was either throwing it away or chucking it down the toilet.

I was in the middle of one of those fake-getting-food trips to the kitchen when I heard my mother talking quietly. That seemed to be the case lately, as she was always on the phone with one of her friends, many of them her "council friends" from Camp Auctus. But she wasn't on the phone nor hologram with anyone. Aunt Emma had come over. Every time we thought Aunt Emma was doing better, she wasn't.

She sat on the couch, her head buried in my mother's shoulder. A movie was on the wall screen, but they weren't really watching. The movie was a distraction. I could hear my aunt sniffling and blowing her nose. "I don't think I can do it," she was saying. "The primaries are coming up, and I have to make a decision but my heart's not into it, Becca."

"I understand. I totally understand," my mom replied.

I tiptoed into the kitchen and into our walk-in pantry. Maybe if I surrounded myself with shelves full of snacks, they would enter my body through osmosis and stay in my system. But mostly, I wanted to hear what Aunt Emma was saying.

"I have nothing to fight for. My entire reason for wanting to make this world a better place is gone. Just gone." She sniffed.

"Not your entire reason," my mom said, caressing her hair. "You still have us. We need you. The country needs you."

"You know what I mean."

"I do." My mom and aunt sat staring at the wall screen. Two people were talking in a bookstore, a man with floppy hair that looked to be the bookshop keeper and a woman with a beret. The man was clearly in love with the woman after just meeting her for the first time.

"I don't know how you're handling this, Emma."

"I'm not. At least you have Julia. She's such a special girl, you know. Did you know she was writing a book during summer camp? A book, Becca! How many twelve-year-olds do you know who are able to write a few pages, much less an entire book?" Aunt Emma gushed.

"I know," my mom agreed, which warmed my broken heart. "I don't think she realizes how special she is. I'm worried about her."

Aunt Emma didn't catch onto that last one. She'd been on her own mind track lately. "Did you also know that she and Lizzie were going to do a video series?" she added, perking up with interest. "They were going to talk about whatever their little hearts desired. Lizzie was going to do life hacks, and Julia review books or something like that. I loved that they were going to do that together."

"No, I didn't know."

"It was all Lizzie could talk about on the bus while we were on the road. She had the first video all planned out. She wanted to talk about 'Surviving a Boring Summer,' she said." She giggled through her tears. My mom laughed too. "She wanted Julia to talk about her biggest influence in life. She thought that would make a first good video, enough to give people a taste of who they were."

"Our daughters are so talented," Mom said. I bit my lip and held in tears.

"Your daughter is," Aunt Emma said. "Mine…"

She broke into a fresh round of sobs again. I knew what she didn't have the courage to say. Mine *was* talented.

I knew what to do. One way or another, I had to try again, because I couldn't stand to see Aunt Emma step down from the presidential race. My mom was right—we needed her. There was no one as qualified as she was. Maybe if she knew what Lizzie had done at the rally, that Lizzie had saved a boy from dying.

I grabbed a granola bar from the shelf, bolted through the kitchen announcing my presence as though I'd just arrived, "Hi, Mom. Hi, Aunt Emma," and blasted back up the stairs. Then I threw the granola bar into my dresser drawer, where eighteen other unopened granola bars awaited consumption, and got my camera set up.

I set up a green screen, so I could use any background I wanted during the editing process. I wiped my tears, wrote up a few lines of script, then decided I needed to do this without one. If I wanted it to be sincere, on the spot, I had to ad-lib it. Only then would anyone understand the truth of my words, feel the only emotion I had left.

Fluff my hair.

Check lighting.

Set camera to record in 3...2...1...

"Hello and welcome to my channel," I said proudly. I tried to imagine Lizzie with me, urging me on, telling me to smile.

I want people to know the Julia I know.

"Many of you don't know me, but my name is Julia. I would be doing this video with my cousin, Elizabeth, who I grew up with. She was like a sister to me, the sister I never had. Neither of us had other siblings. Anyway, she couldn't make it here today. She couldn't make it today, because...well...because someone stole her life."

I stared into the camera, imagining all the people watching this, all the people who never got to know her as I did. I didn't want to talk about how she died, because that would only highlight her death and give satisfaction to all the angry, mentally sick people out there who hated their lives so much, who felt they needed to take others down with them. I would talk about them another day.

Today, I wanted to talk about a hero.

TWENTY

I may not have known his name, but I called him Yugi because of his online handle. He said it was based on an old Japanese card game. Apparently, Yugi was into old Japanese movies, games, and books in a style called *anime* that was supposedly the origins of lots of styles we have today in 2039.

Anyway, I was online with him all the time now. If I wasn't at school, I was locked in my room with Yugi's chat thread on the holoscreen while I either did homework or edited my video about Lizzie. The video turned out okay. I wouldn't say great, because I seemed to be born without the critical gene for entertaining people. My voice sounded flat, and my face could only hold my own attention for seconds at a time.

But…

I put my heart into it. Every last drop of love.

Yugi said it was amazing. He said it brought out the beautiful things about Lizzie that nobody knew, which made me happy. He told me I should add effects and edit out the boring parts, and it would be a good video to share, because the message was great. The message being: *she died too damn soon.*

If Lizzie were still in the world, she'd be painting it different colors, giving it a dazzly, sparkly, glittery coat all while solving people's problems. She excelled at that, which was why people trusted her. Unlike others in this world, whenever she said she was going to do something, she actually did it. I had no doubt we'd be knee deep in creating these videos together today if she was still here.

Lizzie would've made a good presidential candidate.

Too bad we'd never see that happen. She was in the wrong place at the wrong time, and I still don't know who to blame for that. But someone *is* to blame, because kids should feel safe, and my inner fire of rage wouldn't rest until I figured it out.

You know what I like about it?

Yugi asked.

What?

You made her seem like a hero, not because of anything supernatural, but just by being her normal self. I've watched other tributes to victims these last few months. People don't know how to process grief so they say super nice things. They inflate the memory of the dead to a point where they seemed almost like saints. Am I making sense?

I clicked off the editing program to reread his message a few times before nodding.

I think so. You mean I kept it real?

Yes. That. Really powerful.

Thanks,

I smiled, just as my mother knocked on the door and opened it to poke her face through.

"Hi."

"Hi."

"Everything okay?"

"Yes, why?"

I said.

"Nothing, just asking."

"Okay."

"Okay. Dinner's in an hour."

"Fine, thanks," I replied and waited for her to close the door. I sighed before resuming my chat with Yugi. Mom had been doing that every day now for a week. Didn't she realize there was nothing for us to talk about? We lived in two different orbits.

For days now, I hadn't seemed so alone. I had someone to share the darkness with, someone who'd been at the rally instead of me, which made me feel closer to Lizzie somehow. Yugi's memory served as my eyes and ears of a place I would only ever imagine. To be honest, if my mom had said I could go to the rally and I'd been there to see Lizzie get killed, I wasn't sure I'd ever come out of that darkness.

My heart ached for anyone who'd ever gone through that, the school shootings, the public massacres, or even non-public ones. My God, how did they cope? How could someone unsee what they'd seen? Yes, I felt grateful for having been safely out of the way, but on the other, I should've been there to help. To protect her. I might've pushed her safely out of the way the way she'd done to Yugi.

So many questions I'd never have answers to.

I finished the video and chatted with my new buddy some more while it rendered. When the chiming noise signaled it was done, I shared it with him. Funny I was showing it to a total stranger, a boy with a fake name and no face, before anyone else. But I trusted Yugi. I had always been a good judge of character, which was why I'd only had one good friend in all my life.

I waited the whole ten minutes while he watched it. He replied with simply this:

You have to share that. With the world.

It's not perfect and my face looks like a potato

I replied.

It doesn't. It's a nice face.

That one made me blush. For the first time, I wondered what Yugi looked like.

Doesn't have to be perfect, he added. You said what you needed to say.

Not completely. There's so much more I want to say about the tragedy but I don't know how to put it into words. Like, for months now, I'm just…angry. Not only because of my cousin's death but at…I don't know…the world. Adults. I don't know if that's even fair, so I don't say it.

I get it, he replied. You feel like a whole generation failed you.

YES. EXACTLY THAT,

I typed back.

Has your aunt seen it?

he asked.

No.

It might make her happy.

I thought about it. Would it make Aunt Emma even sadder, or brighten her day? At the end of the day, she was just a mother who missed her child, and this could cheer her up. I decided that yes, it'd put a smile on her face. I sent it off to my aunt, along with my hopes and prayers that she'd take it the right way, wishing the sight of all the photos of Lizzie I'd included wouldn't drive her deeper into grief.

I waited for her to reply, while Yugi made me laugh with stories about his friends at school. This kid really understood all the sides of this complicated problem when nobody else in my family did. Part of me wanted to share him with my parents, tell them, *Look, here's somebody who understands what I'm feeling.* But another part of me wanted to keep him a secret.

Keep him mine, pure and real, forever.

A week passed, and I hadn't heard back from Aunt Emma. She must've hated it. I must've spoken too angrily about the shooting. Something I noticed was that people could feel angry after a tragedy, but if the families of victims talked too much about it, after a while people stopped listening. They wanted to move on and not think about it anymore.

Also, Aunt Emma might've still felt like Lizzie's death had been her fault. It was never my intention to remind her of that. I only talked about how there should be stricter laws to prevent this sort of thing from happening ever again. I thought she'd appreciate that because it sounded like the stuff she'd said during her campaign.

Each day, I second-guessed myself a little more. I shouldn't have sent it.

Now it was out there. And I couldn't get it back.

At the dinner table, things were quieter than usual. Mom's eyelids sagged at the corners and I thought I noticed new wrinkles. She hadn't looked her usual youthful self in a while. Crying did that to a person, dehydrate a person's face. My dad acted like everything was fine. He just dug into his food with gusto, while my mom and I mostly pushed the morsels around on our plates.

Had Mom seen the video? She'd been acting strange, coming into my room each day, as though hoping I'd break into spontaneous conversation with her. Could that be why she was so quiet at the table? The thought crossed my mind like a cold breeze snaking through an open window. Maybe Aunt Emma had watched my video about Lizzie, disapproved of it, and shown it to my mother. I should've shared it with her first to get her opinion. Maybe they both hated it.

"Are you okay?" Mom asked, giving me a quick glance between bites of food.

My stomach started its signature hurt. "Yes, why do you keep asking me that?" I may have replied a bit too bluntly.

"Because you haven't eaten anything, Jules. You don't talk to me when you used to talk to me, and you look tired."

"YOU look tired," I fired back. *Whoa*, not a good move.

"Jules." My father set down his fork and stared at me.

"No, it's okay," Mom said to him, holding out her hand. "We need to talk. As a family. Or we'll never know what's going on."

"Going on with what? There's nothing going on," I said, shoving a bite of sweet potatoes into my mouth. It felt like a gray, bland mass. "Just please let me eat."

My mother's sigh was barely audible, but I felt it in my toes. "I haven't had a conversation with my daughter since before the summer."

"But then came the summer," I mumbled.

"Julia," my father warned.

"Yes? Dad?" I said as calmly as possible. "It's true. Summer changed everything, did it not?"

"It did. But we are still a family," Mom said. "And you're in your room all day, you mope to school, mope back, we never see you, and you eat...very little. We want you to share what you're feeling."

"Maybe if you stopped asking me how I'm doing all the time."

"Maybe if you shared what you're going through, I wouldn't have to ask," Mom bit back.

"That makes no sense," I muttered.

"So...what you're saying is...if I stop talking to you, you'll talk to me then?" Mom tossed her napkin into her lap. "Because I'm willing to try whatever it takes."

"Yes. But you know what else would be great?" I bit my lip and forced to keep from uttering another word before I'd regret it. "...is if you just left me alone."

There, I'd said it. Now I'd become the callous, insensitive teenager she was making me out to be. This was a lose-lose situation. I got up, took my plate to the sink, and started leaving the kitchen.

"Nobody said you could go, Julia. Sit down so we can work this out," my father ordered.

I couldn't stay and pretend like nothing was wrong.

I kept walking. "There's nothing to say. We're the same happy family as always. Nothing to see here. Keep moving like life is perfectly normal!" I ran to the stairs and bolted up before my dad had the chance to say anything else, tears stinging my eyes.

"Julia!" Mom called.

"Just let her be," Dad quietly told her.

I charged up the stairs into my room, careful not to slam the door. I had no intention of being difficult or dramatic, I just wanted them to leave me alone to handle things my own way. My way did not entail awkward conversation about it over sweet potatoes and steak. At least here I didn't have to pretend that all was fine when in truth, my entire world had fallen apart. In my room, I could be me. Whoever that was. I didn't know anymore.

I sat at my desk and typed a message to Yugi:

Are you there?

No response. Maybe he was having dinner also.

I feel like throwing up. I've been throwing up every day for the last few months. At first I just couldn't keep food down, but now I think I do it on purpose. I can keep food down or I can bring it up, unlike other stuff I can't control.

Anyway...Earth to Mars...

Pushing my chair back, I flew to the bathroom, closed the door, and knelt in front of the toilet. What little I'd eaten came frothing back up. The same strange thought I'd had other times returned to haunt me—*if Lizzie can't eat, then I won't either.* I may not have been able to apply the same rule to living, because I didn't have a choice on that one, but with food, I had control.

When I reopened the bathroom door and stepped into my room, my mom stood there, hunched over the computer, reading my message to Yugi. When she heard me, she pulled off her glasses and straightened, a concerned look on her face. "Who is this you're talking to? And what does all this mean?"

Ugh...great.

For the next couple of months, I visited Dr. Aileen Merida, a behavioral therapist specializing in eating disorders. Twice a week. She told me to call her Dr. Aileen. At first, I was mad my parents made me go. I told them I could stop throwing up on my own whenever I wanted. I could gain the twenty pounds back.

But Dr. Aileen wasn't that bad. She was young and had suffered from bulimia as a teen, so she understood. She said all my behaviors were normal for someone who'd lost a sibling or family member. Apparently, I was trying to cope with the trauma the only way I knew how and did not want to unnecessarily upset my parents, which was why I kept the vomiting a secret. And yes, controlling what I ate or didn't eat helped me feel less powerless to the hand the universe had dealt me.

One of the first things she had me do was start a journal, which I liked because it was writing. But the next exercise was harder—facing my fears. She told me, when I was ready, I should go to Lizzie's house, see her room, see her box of lucky treasures, revisit the spots where we'd played for so many years. I needed to see her bed, her unicorn curtains, her stuffed animals in the bookcase. She said I needed closure, the satisfaction that something has ended.

Closure. Like closing a door. Or a chapter.

I knew in my heart, especially after seeing the box marked "LIZZIE CAMP" sitting in her bedroom against the wall, though, that I'd never get "closure." I'd always feel like Lizzie should still be here. Still, it made me cry a ton, sitting on edge of her bed inside her bright yellow room. Something about that did make me feel better.

After I came back downstairs to find Grandma Wendy talking to Mom, they both asked, "Do you need anything, Jules?" Not "what's wrong?" or "why won't you tell us what you're feeling?" Two questions I could never answer. But "Do you need anything?" The change of question made all the difference in the world. Because yes—I needed their love and support. And patience.

And I would need it for the next few years.

Around the same time, the video went viral. It was even used in school social studies classes. I guess because a lot of what I said echoed my aunt's opinions before "the incident," when she used to hold rallies and go around giving speeches, like she did at Camp Auctus. I talked about needing even stricter laws on guns, about a tragedy before my mom was born called Columbine, one of the first school shootings in the U.S. and how kids shouldn't have to wait sixty years to get the protection we need.

The video even pissed off President Walker, who supposedly watched it and told me I should stick to what I knew as a twelve-year-old, stuff like kissing boys and doing makeup, not talking about gun control. What twelve-year-old went around kissing boys? Showed how out of touch he was with my generation, the most cautious of any of the last four. This unreasonable madman was what my Aunt Emma was up against.

But instead of fighting, my aunt took a month off, during which time I never heard if she liked the video about Lizzie or not. I think it was too painful for her to watch. She went to the west coast of Florida and sat on a beach for, like, weeks. It was like watching your favorite superhero get drunk off beer and cry on the couch all day.

Finally, one day, she showed up at our house, and I trudged downstairs to find her in the kitchen with everyone surrounding her.

"There she is." When Aunt Emma smiled, something in me wanted to cry. Her arms opened up big and she took me in. I'd missed her.

"Hey, Aunt Emma." I hugged her so hard. It felt good. We both needed it. "Where you've been?"

"I needed a break. But I want you know that because of your video, I'm back."

"You're back...question mark?" I narrowed my eyes, unsure of what she meant.

"Back on the campaign trail. Jules, I couldn't watch it at first. But everyone insisted I needed to." She rested her palm against my cheek. "Thank you for making it. After watching it, how could I say no?"

"To what?" I asked, as my mom and dad exchanged glances.

"To running for president. It's all because of you."

TWENTY-ONE

I heard the laughter, the voice crooning through the megaphone, the bells and sounds of girls racing each other. Someone shook my leg who felt suspiciously like Cassie. "Wake up, Julia," she said near my ear. "We're headed to the mess hall for lunch."

I rubbed my eyes. "What time is it?"

"Lunch time, obviously. Ms. Caroline told me to come wake you. Come on, author."

"Okay…"

How long had I slept? For a moment, I forgot where I was. I opened my eyes to see the bright sun-filled quarters of the Writer's Hut and had to think hard to remind myself—Camp Auctus, end of summer, 2041. I was here to write a speech about Lizzie for the ceremony tomorrow, but I'd spent a week isolated in this cabin to finish my novel instead.

"Is she coming?" I heard one of the girls outside the cabin's open windows.

"She'll meet us there," Cassie replied without much hope.

I felt the usual twinge of guilt all over again, the one I'd been feeling since I'd returned to camp a couple weeks ago. Maybe it was time to meet up with these girls, be one of the group for once. Move on and rejoin the outside world.

I changed quickly, tucked my half-heart charm into my shirt, slipped a brush through my tangled rat's nest of hair, and rushed over to the mess hall. I may have sacrificed the last couple of meals, and my stomach rumbled like a sneaker inside a clothes dryer, but I'd finally finished my book. Of that I felt entirely proud. Me, a regular fourteen-year-old had finished a *novel*.

Around two in the morning, I'd also decided on a new title, too—*Summer Taken*.

I smiled. That was an accomplishment no one could take from me.

When I walked into the mess hall, most of my cabin mates (if I could still call them that after I'd spent so many days alone) were in line for the buffet. Cassie and Tori actually waved me over and let me skip in front of them. That was nice of them, considering I'd been holed up by myself for most of my two-week stay, but now we were ahead of Tinay and Naomi, whose stares I still found difficult to ignore.

"How's it going in the Writer's Hut?" Cassie asked. "Did you finish your book yet?"

"I actually did." I shrugged.

"Really? Wow, congrats, Julia. That's so cool." Cassie clapped her fingertips together.

"Thanks. It's kind of hard to believe." I smiled back at Tori whose face was serving me looks of being thoroughly impressed.

"Maybe now you can help us with chores."

I looked behind me at whoever said it.

Tinay stood there with her arms crossed, giving me a smug look. Something about that girl would forever intimidate me. "Because you know what today is, right?" she asked, eyebrows raised expectantly.

"Yes, mandatory cabin cleanup," I replied. "I haven't forgotten."

"Full inspection," she added. "*Everybody* should help."

"Yeah. I definitely will," I replied carefully. "I planned on it."

"Oh, had you?"

Cassie gave Tinay an edgy glare, like it was time to shut the hell up.

Tori, in her diplomatic way, excused Tinay's snide remark. "She's just kidding," she laughed nervously. "We just wish we would see more of you, Julia. We've hardly seen you since you came back."

I didn't think that's what Tinay meant, but it was nice of Tori to try and diffuse the tension.

"I know, I'm sorry." I moved up in line. "I guess I've been trying to figure my life out. Also, I've been thinking about it and...I think I want to come back next year. From the start of camp, this time. I've come to Camp Auctus for the beginning of summer, then the end of summer, but I've never stayed the *whole* summer. It's time."

I couldn't believe the words coming out of my own mouth. "Will you guys be here?"

"Yeah, I'll be here," Cassie said.

"Me too, unless my parents are doing their 'Great American Road Trip,'" Tori laughed.

"Good. I'm going to tell Ms. Caroline today." Yes, I was ready to experience Camp Auctus the way I

176

should have from the start. I liked to think perhaps Lizzie was nudging me forward, a little angel on my shoulder. I smiled, as Cassie and Tori both nodded their approval. "I think I owe it to Elizabeth to start over. You know?"

Cassie and Tori both nodded. "We agree, Julia. Lizzie would want you to have fun."

These girls really did want to be friends with me. I should've given them the chance earlier, like Lizzie had said.

"Totally awesome," Tinay mumbled. "You'll come back for another summer, and Ms. Caroline will give you more special privileges. You'll write Book 2 while the rest of us slave away."

"Huh?" I turned to face her. It was no surprise that was how Tinay saw me—a teacher's pet, a butt-kisser, a fragile little girl who needed special care. I may have been quiet most of the time, but I was still stressed and still not in the mood to take crap from anyone.

"You heard me," Tinay said, her hazel eyes zeroed in on me.

"Believe me, I'd rather be cleaning a cabin than dealing with a loved one's death," I stammered. "Do you want to switch places with me, Tinay?"

She scoffed. "I'm not saying it doesn't suck. Look, I'm sorry. But after two years? You should be fine now."

"Seriously?" Tori gaped at her. A few girls in line ahead of us turned to gawk as well.

"Yes, Tori. Seriously. The camp administrators are only having the ceremony because it's Elizabeth Richards, daughter of—"

"You know what?" Cassie got right into Tinay's face. "You need to stop."

"It's been two years, Cass. The best way to get over losing someone is to let go completely. The more you hold onto the pain, the harder it is to let go."

I was about to protest when I saw something in Tinay's eyes. She sounded like someone who knew what she was talking about. Like she'd been through this. And like Dr. Aileen said—we all cope in different ways. I would've asked her about her experience, but I remembered what it was like when everybody would ask me questions all the time. Tinay would talk about it whenever she was ready.

We slid down the row, picking up rolls, salads, and pasta dishes.

"That might work for you, but not for me," I said. "I have a different way of coping. I write everything out." Everyone looked at me like I had a cat on top of my head.

I was unafraid of talking to her at this point. Oddly enough, I felt brave, strong, capable of standing up for myself. Without Lizzie there to help. Without Cassie. Tinay was just another person, nobody to feel scared about. She'd been through pain, too.

"Yeah," Cassie backed me up. "So leave her alone."

Maybe it was because I'd finally spoken aloud, but that was the end of that. Tinay didn't antagonize me anymore. We were done. We could move on now.

Cassie and Tori gave their lunch numbers to the mess hall cashier, while I stood there waiting to give my number, happy with the way I'd handled that. I never did possess that quality of being able to move on from a difficult situation, brush it off, and stay friends, but that was probably because I'd never tried.

Lizzie would've been proud of me.

The director's office door was ajar again, like it was the day I walked in and saw Ms. Caroline sobbing into the phone. Seeing it that way gave me shivers. Today, she was filling out forms on the computer, and Ms. Susan was making a pot of coffee from the good coffeemaker they kept in the back of their office.

"Hello, Ms. Caroline, Ms. Susan," I said, holding on to the doorframe. "Ms. Caroline, I finished my book."

"You did?" Her bright eyes lit up.

"Yes. Two hundred pages total." I smiled.

"The great author, Julia Weissman! I want the first copy when it's published. You hear me?" She beamed like she always did.

I would give my family the first copies, of course, but I nodded, because she was only being nice. "Of course. Hey, Ms. Caroline, I'm going to help the girls clean the cabin for inspection today. Just wanted you to know. Also, I wanted to tell you that…well, I think I want to come next year."

Her brown eyes lit up with excitement. "Oh, Julia. That's the best news I've heard all day." She got out of her seat to come hug me. "I will make sure it's your best year ever. Also, I'm putting together the program for tomorrow. I don't mean to hurry you, but are you going to write a tribute? It's okay if you aren't. I just need to know if to include you in the program or not. No pressure, dear."

"I'll try," I said.

Ms. Caroline hung there watching me carefully. Sometimes I felt she could read minds. "Ms. Susan," she said without taking her eyes off me. "Could you give Julia and me a minute?"

"Sure." Ms. Susan grabbed a stack of files sitting on top of the file cabinet and headed out of the office past me. "See you girls later," she said in her sing-songy voice.

Ms. Caroline gestured to an empty, half-busted chair. "Sit for a second."

"Okay." I sat.

"It's been so frantic around here, what with all the parents arriving tomorrow and all, but I wanted to tell you how very proud of you I am."

"For what?"

"You know. For the way you've been handling your time here. Also, the last two years. I know it hasn't been easy, but maybe this will be a turning point for you. At Camp Auctus, we pride ourselves with giving young women the opportunity to be themselves, to give them space, while also the tools to become the leaders they were destined to become."

"You sound like a brochure, Ms. Caroline."

"Oh, Julia." Her shoulders deflated a little. "I planted an envelope inside the Writer's Hut desk. It's from Elizabeth. She gave it to me the last day I saw her. I've kept it all this time. Didn't want to burden you anymore than you already were by mailing it to your home. Your mother has kept me up to date on your progress."

"You mean my eating disorder therapy."

"Yes, dear. I know it's been a hard road. And I need to be honest—I've read Elizabeth's letter to you.

So has your mother. Ultimately, we had to decide if it was something you were ready for."

They both read it? "Only I can decide that, Ms. Caroline."

"Right you are. That's why I sealed it back up, didn't mention it, and put it in the desk. I thought perhaps if you found it yourself, it would settle something inside your soul. Perhaps you'd feel inspired to write about her. Not for the speech—I'll support whatever you decide—but because I thought you might find peace. Closure."

There was that word again.

It'd been two years, and I still hadn't found this "closure" thing, but she was right—maybe I needed to stop being afraid of everything and just read the letter already. "I will," I sighed. "I'll read it tonight."

"Good." She smiled, wandered over to her desk, and opened the drawer. She looked into it longingly, then closed it back up. "I don't think you'll be disappointed by it. Your cousin had a talent for bringing a smile to people's faces. You're a special girl, Julia. I have been honored to know you these last two years."

"Thank you, Ms. Caroline. Were you going to give me something from that drawer?"

"No, dear. Just thinking. I have to get back to work, but let me know if there's anything else you need."

"I will. Thank you."

I left her office with an oddly settled feeling in my soul, like everything was finally falling into place. I would be okay. Maybe Pastor Bryan was right and time really did heal all wounds, even ones as painful as mine. Whatever Lizzie's letter said, I could handle it. I could move on from it. She was twelve when she wrote it. I was older now and more mature.

I stopped by the Writer's Hut to fish out the little pink envelope from inside the desk. Flipping it over in my hands, I traced Lizzie's handwriting with my fingertip, grabbed a blanket, and headed to the lake while other girls worked on their performances for our Summer's End Show.

I planted my butt on mine and Lizzie's favorite spot. With a whopping breath, I slid my finger underneath the glued edge of the letter, unfolded the stationery, and with my heart in my throat, began to read…

TWENTY-TWO

Dear Julia,

Ms. Caroline told me I should try writing you a handwritten letter. She said the art of writing by hand has been lost but it's a powerful way of connecting with someone. So, here I am—writing to a talented writer. I feel so self-conscious, ha ha.

I know you're really pissed at me right now, but I have to do this. Julia, you're your best when you're inside, creating, quietly writing words. I'm at my best when I'm outside, meeting people and talking. It's a miracle we even get along, we're so different. But we are like Aunt Becca and my mom, except kids instead of moms.

What's great about us is...you make me better. I make you better.

Together we're unstoppable!

I know I asked you to come to Camp Auctus with me, and I know you didn't want to, so <u>thank you</u> for coming even though I made you a little uncomfortable. Okay, a lot uncomfortable. I know you did it for me. I love you! If my mom hadn't surprised me yesterday, I would've stayed and completed my amazing summer with you. You know that.

But my mom did surprise me. And I had been

praying for a long time for her to have more time with me. This year has been sooo hard. Because she's the Senator, I don't get to see her much. Some kids would be fine without their moms around, but I've always needed more time with mine. She works so hard. For us. For other people. For our state. So whenever she makes time just for me, yeah I guess I jump at that opportunity.

I'm not sorry for that. But I am sorry that you feel I'm abandoning you. I'm not. I'm always with you, no matter where I am in the world. Just sit by the lake and you'll hear me laughing. Run past the row of pines and you'll hear me gasping for air because I can never keep up with you. Walk into the theater and you'll hear me saying my lines.

Julia, I want you to be happy without me there. Please. I hate the thought that whenever I leave your side, you're sad, and whenever I ask you to try something new, you get scared. I know it's "who you are," but I know it's also fear you're feeling. Take a chance and you'll see it'll all be fine! There's so many cool things in the world to try! I mean, that's why we're alive, isn't it?

I introduced you to the Writer's Hut so you could be happy, but I also wanted you to make friends—make all the friends! Make the girls love Julia Weissman the way I love her. Show them the amazing person you are inside. The thunderstorm that is me may be leaving for a little while, but the soothing rain that is you is just as important (Grandma Wendy said that to me—I can't take credit).

I love you, Jules. It's all going to be okay. I promise.

I'll write to you from the road, then I'll see you at home. We'll do those videos and rule the world together, okay? Elizabeth 'n' Julia for-EVAH!!!!!

Love you,
Lizzie

I folded the letter and let it drop in my lap.

I should've known her personality would leap off the paper. Maybe that's what I'd been afraid of all this time, hearing her voice again. It was hard enough not being able to see her anymore, but reading her handwriting and hearing her words in my head was almost more than I could bear. But I was grateful.

"Miss you, silly girl."

My eyes filled with swirly, watery tears that made the lake look like a Monet painting under the sparkling sun. Funny thing was, I *could* hear her laughing. I *could* hear her gasping for breath trying to catch up with me. If I listened closely enough, I *could* hear her reciting her lines.

Lizzie would always be around. As long as I kept her alive in my mind and my heart, she lived. She thrived. Multiply that vitality times all the people who had ever loved her, and her spirit would live forever. I could feel her presence even now sitting next to Lake Bradford.

I knew everything I wanted to say about her at the remembrance tomorrow.

I didn't even have to write it down.

It was all right here—in my heart.

I could tell it was the last day of camp from the

reverberations of the sound system being tested in the amphitheater and the fact that my cabin mates were all scrambling to pack their things. Upon waking, we got straight to work, getting dressed, finishing up our packing, cleaning the cabin, and polishing off the Camp Auctus look with the signature green ribbons in our hair.

Today was the day.

My mother would be here soon to fawn over me, take a million pics, and then camp, the two weeks I'd been here, would be over. Off to high school with us. Another chapter in my life gone. While I could only hope that normalcy might resume, I knew it wouldn't. Not the old normalcy. But hopefully, a new one. Writing about my summer two years ago in the Writer's Hut really helped me get a lot off my chest. I realized I wasn't the only one suffering.

My mom had suffered. My dad. Grandma Wendy, Granddad, Aunt Emma.

All of us in different ways, but we'd all suffered the loss of a beautiful soul.

After lunch, campers gathered in the amphitheater. Most of the girls buzzed with excitement as we waited for Ms. Caroline to begin, while I breathed in and out deeply and hoped I wouldn't mess this up. At 1 PM on the dot, she and Ms. Susan shuffled onto the stage to applause and whistles from the crowd. I sat bouncing my knees and chewing my fingernails.

Cassie tapped my shoulder to make me chill.

"Sorry," I muttered. "Nervous."

"You'll do great." Cassie gave me a sweet smile. "I know you will."

"Thanks." I gave her one back. It was nice to

know I wasn't a complete loner and had a couple of friends on my side—*The Lizzie-less Starter Set*. The true test would be keeping in touch with them after we all went home to our separate corners of the world.

"Good morning, campers. Good morning, parents. Welcome to our closing ceremonies." Ms. Caroline waved at the crowd. "I think this summer was the fastest eight weeks yet. Thank you for letting us spend this time with your children. It is such a privilege for us that you entrust us with your girls for this brief but important time in their lives."

Nods scattered across the amphitheater. I couldn't find my mother anywhere, but I knew she was out there in the sea of faces.

"We'd like to take a moment to thank the illustrious alumni in our audience," Ms. Caroline said. She named several people, a few I'd heard of before. "Amaal Thomas and Lucy Vidrine, the architects of the U.S.-Iran Accord, which resulted in normalizing relations between the two countries just over a decade ago."

The names Amaal and Lucy sounded familiar. I was almost certain they were friends of my mother's. As the audience applauded, two beautiful women stood and waved. Yes, I was pretty sure I'd seen their photos before.

Ms. Caroline and Ms. Susan spent some time going over official closing business and announcements, and with every passing moment, I grew more and more nervous. Soon I'd be called up to give my speech about Elizabeth.

I had no idea how people did this, how Lizzie ever relished public speaking. This was easily the most nerve-wracking thing I'd ever done. Cassie had to tap my knee again to stop it from bouncing.

"Sorry," I whispered and chewed on my lower lip.

Ms. Susan's voice was strong and melodious compared to Ms. Caroline's soft and sweet one. "We are looking forward to seeing you back here next summer. For our fifteen-year-olds, if you're interested in becoming counselors-in-training next year, please check the guidelines on our website in a week or two, after we've settled down a bit. And now, without further ado, the 2041 Camp Auctus Summer's End Show. Hit it, ladies!"

I watched my camp mates sing, dance, cheer, do monologues, even have a hot debate onstage. Parents laughed, cheered, and took turns crowding the aisles, all to get that perfect social media shot. After forty minutes of performances, it was my turn to start making my way backstage. I was to go onstage after Brianna's guitar performance of "Blowin' in the Wind," a song she told us was symbolic of the changes in our country eighty years ago.

After she finished, everyone stood to applaud her, and dread spread in my stomach. Ms. Caroline nodded to me before walking out onstage to make sure I was ready. I wasn't. I'd never be ready. But I took Lizzie's letter to heart. *Take risks. Get out in the world.*

Make her proud.

"And now, ladies and gentlemen, we have a special commemoration. You may have noticed we have a new formal garden. Our next presenter is the daughter and niece of a pair of ladies who attended Camp Auctus many moons ago—her mother, Rebecca

Miller-Weissman, and aunt, Emma Singletary-Richards."

The place broke into applause then died down quickly when Ms. C shushed them. "As did her grandmother and great-grandmother. A family of strong, talented women, I assure you. You may recognize her as the face of the viral video, 'My Cousin, My Hero.' She'll be saying a few words about Elizabeth Richards, whom we were blessed to know as well. Please welcome Miss Julia Weissman!"

Ms. Caroline waved me on.

This was it.

I closed my eyes, breathed in enough air to let the oxygen seep into my muscles and relax me, then walked onto the stage to applause followed by a stoic silence. A few people coughed. Ms. Caroline welcomed me with a big hug, patted me gently, then moved off to the side. While I stood there thinking about the words I'd practiced all morning, I could see her in my peripheral vision. I was grateful for her presence.

The amphitheater was silent.

I stared at the faces staring back at me, well-meaning parents smiling and nodding, encouraging me not to be frightened, to speak from the heart. Flitting my gaze around, I caught my mother's oval face and pretty eyebrows just off center. Next to her was Dad and...was that Granddad and Grandma? But I thought only Mom was flying up to get me. Seeing my family's smiles calmed my pounding heart, and I inhaled deeply once more before pulling the microphone closer to my mouth.

Of course, it screeched.

"Thanks, Ms. Caroline." I cleared my throat.

My voice was shaky. I inhaled a few more times. The exhale made me sound like a mouth-breather in the microphone. "Like she said, I'm Julia. Many of you might not know me, even though I came to camp two years ago. I've also been here the last two weeks, but you still might not have seen me. I keep mostly to myself."

A deeper lull settled over the audience. I heard more coughs and even a few hushed giggles, but I couldn't worry about it now.

"Two years ago, I came to Camp Auctus excited. It was my first summer here. I'd never been to any camp before, but my cousin Lizzie told me about all the fun stuff there was to do here. I had no idea just how special this place would be. A lot of history. A lot of tradition. It can be overwhelming. So many amazing women have walked these same trails, slept in these same cabins. I was terrified. I had huge shoes to fill.

"After years of telling me how awesome camp was, Lizzie finally convinced me to join her. I'll be honest. People are not my thing."

A few giggles bubbled through the amphitheater.

"I'm an introvert and not one of those extrovert-introverts either. I don't do well in groups, never have. But Lizzie had so much she wanted to show me, so I said okay. I'll go. And we had the most amazing time. I spent a lot of time in the Writer's Hut, but at least I was out of my house and comfort zone. Little by little, she got me to participate in stuff.

"But then, she had to go. I was heartbroken."

I scanned the crowd, expecting to see some smirks from Tinay's friends, but everyone was listening. They all knew the story.

"I'll get straight to the point. That summer, my cousin was killed. By a gunman."

Silence in the audience. Sad faces peered back at me.

"She left camp for an election rally with her mom, because who wouldn't want to be with their mom, right?" I added. I did *not* want to make Aunt Emma any more sad than she already was.

I scanned the audience for her again, seeing a group of men and women dressed in black hanging off to the side.

"Especially Lizzie. She would've followed her mom to the moon, if she could have. That's how much she loved her." I connected with Aunt Emma in the audience. Her eyes were red, but she was smiling.

"Still, I got mad at her for leaving, and I didn't understand why at the time. I just felt like it wasn't fair. But that was me, thinking of my own sadness. I wasn't seeing the bigger picture. I wasn't thinking about her happiness." I swallowed down tears.

"The thing is, I didn't know anyone. That was my fault. I didn't think I could survive without her." My voice trembled. I swallowed hard. "Turns out that 'surviving without Lizzie' has been the theme of my life the last two years." I breathed through the rising tears.

Ms. Caroline floated close enough to hand me a tissue. I took it.

"Anyway, I'm supposed to tell you about Lizzie, not the tragedy, and I will, but I can't stand here and not tell you what's really been hurting the last two years besides her dying. It's how nothing good ever comes of this, of tragic deaths. You think people will learn their lesson. You think things will change, but they don't.

"I understand bad things happen to people. Accidents, not-accidents... You can get in a car in the morning, thinking you're going to see your mom speak at a rally and end up dead in a hospital a day later. Life can change in the blink of an eye. I get that. You can go to war and never return. You can go to school, thinking you're just going to have a test today, and instead it's your last day—ever. Anything can happen."

I was talking. With a few hundred people.

And they were listening. To me.

People dabbed their eyes and nodded.

"The day my cousin went to Aunt Emma's rally, someone decided to break in and take my aunt's life, all because she wants to help people. Because she wants to make the world a better place. Isn't that what senators are supposed to do? But no, this person sprayed bullets everywhere. They didn't care about anyone."

I paused, thinking how I shouldn't go into the details. But they were true, and I couldn't keep silent anymore.

"One of those bullets almost hit someone else. I can't tell you his name, but I can tell you that Lizzie got in the way. She saved him. But that was Lizzie, going around saving the world." I smiled to myself, imagining Lizzie wearing a spandex superhero's costume.

"She was totally a doer. She'd try anything once. She used to get others to try things, too. She wanted other people to see joy the way she saw it. That's because she loved life. I know, that if she'd been allowed to grow up, she would've become president someday."

I watched Aunt Emma press a tissue to her nose.

"But we'll never know who she would've become. And that hurts more than anything. I'll never have my cousin again. I'll never talk with her on the living room sofa like we used to do. I'll never go to her birthday parties, bake cookies, make fun videos, watch movies, walk my dog with her, or anything.

"I'll never see her wedding. Our daughters would've come to this camp together, but now it won't happen. That chain has been broken." I imagined Elizabeth in her twenties, dressing in wedding gown, with me by her side as the maid of honor, helping her with her veil.

Taken.

I imagined us sitting on the floor while our babies played.

Taken.

I blotted my eyes. "Some things can't be prevented and some things can. It's easier to get a gun than it is to get a driver's license." Parents in the audience nodded, while a few crossed their arms.

"I don't know what the answer is. But my aunt is working on it. I feel like she's the only person who cares to make a change, but that makes sense—Lizzie was her daughter. But let's not only care when it's our daughter, though. Let's care as if we're *all* your daughters. I don't want to be afraid in public anymore. Some of the laws are stupid. I can't even bring a water bottle onto an airplane, yet people get to carry guns."

I sensed a division in the crowd, but everyone respectfully listened. Lots of parents nodded and clapped. I could feel their collective support. It wasn't the tightest speech in the world, but it didn't matter. It was from my heart.

"All I'm saying is, there has to be a solution to this. Let's do what we can to really make change. That's what Camp Auctus is about, isn't it? Lizzie was the most beautiful girl I ever knew. She radiated love and light. Anyone who met her saw that. It's in her photos. It's in her videos. You can see it in the way she twirled and danced, in the way she ran through a sprinkler, in the way she delivered a line like she wanted the Academy Award."

The audience giggled.

"In only twelve years, Lizzie became my inspiration. I only wish I'd had more time with her, but I'm grateful for the time I did. Thank you."

I stepped back from the microphone and instinctively tapped on the charm hanging inside my shirt. My ST ENDS.

Everyone cheered wildly, stood, and clapped, while only a few people reluctantly put two hands together. I'm sure they thought I shouldn't have talked about the gun thing, but how could I not? Lizzie would've been here if it hadn't been for guns in the hands of an unstable person. I would never, ever talk about her again without mentioning the part that took her life. I had to honor my cousin's memory. Make her death count for something.

Ms. Caroline stood by me, putting her arm around me while my family took photos of us. "Thank you, Julia. Wise words from someone so young. Thank you so much."

I hugged her and exhaled a big breath.

Once the event was over, my chest expanded

like a balloon being set free from my soul. I'd done it—I'd said my piece, explained why I was both sad and angry, and expressed my feelings of unfairness. There was much hugging, photo taking, and reveling among my camp mates and families. Everyone began heading to the common area, as I searched for my family.

I spotted them over by the amphitheater exit—my parents and grandparents, otherwise known as the Sneaky Ones. "Hey, you didn't tell me you were coming today."

Granddad hugged me hard. "Great job on that speech, honey."

"Thanks, Granddad."

"Yes, so proud of you!" Mom pulled me into an embrace. After a few moments, she stepped back, put her hands on my shoulders, and looked into my eyes. "I know that wasn't easy."

I felt a million different emotions percolating inside. Something in me had changed. After that speech, I might never be afraid to talk in public ever again. I hugged my mom again. I felt safe. Mature. But still like a kid, maybe something in between. I felt mortified and happy all at the same time. I quietly sank into Mom's arms and felt my dad's cover me as well.

"I'm sorry I was mad at you for making me come back to camp. Ms. Caroline let me use the Writer's Hut as much as I wanted, though. I wrote so much, I think my heart exploded."

Mom laughed. "Well, writing has always been your mode of expression, Julia." She patted my back with one hand, then ran it through my hair, then hugged me again, rocking back and forth. She was embarrassing me with all her gushing, but I remembered how my aunt would never be able to feel her own daughter's hugs again, so I let her.

I stepped back. "Ms. Caroline told me a little about your camp days here. Maybe you can tell me more one day."

My mom smiled. "Yes, we did have some adventures. I would like that."

Just then, we were ambushed by a huge group of people. "Amaal! Lucy! Deserae, Samantha…oh my God. We're all together! The Council is here!" Mom jumped from person to person, hugging everybody.

"Except for your stepsister." The one Mom called Deserae took her up in a hug. "That girl is always off somewhere, talking to somebody. Some things never change."

"She'll show up," Mom said, glancing around. "Guys, this is my amazing daughter, Julia."

Everyone gave me high-fives and told me what a great speech it was. Amaal told me to never be afraid of what people think. Just say what's in my heart. I thought that was pretty good advice. She said you could never go wrong if you did that.

Grandma Wendy walked around doling out hugs and pats on the back in her usual former governor's style, but then she'd always been the friendly type. It was so nice to see her happy and in her element. "Dr. Samantha, Judge Tiffany, so good to see you! So marvelous to see you all with your partners and children."

Watching my mom with all her friends made me wonder where *my* life was headed. Would I become a public speaker? Or stick with writing? I still loved the idea of living on Mars one day. Maybe I'd run Camp

Auctus.

Tori and Cassie came shimmying up to me with shock in their grins. "Oh, my God! How on Earth did you do that, Julia? Even I can't do that!"

Cassie laughed as we formed a little circle, just the three of us. I imagined Lizzie there with us, listening and laughing. "I know, right? I don't think I've heard you utter so many words the whole two weeks you've been here, girl!"

"Thanks. I know it wasn't perfect, but…"

"Trust me," Cassie said, eyes wide. "It was perfect. You should've seen some of the people in the audience. I was cheering inside my head. My mom always says, if you don't have enemies, you're not standing up for anything. Or something like that."

"Luckily, I don't care if I have enemies," I said and felt a heavy weight lift off my shoulders.

Speaking of which, Tinay and Naomi walked past just then with a few of their friends. Normally, I would've looked the other way in fear of what might transpire, but this time I just nodded at them. Tinay nodded back. "Nice speech, President Julia." She gave me a totally sincere smile so wide, my heart leaped into the air.

Make friends. Make all the friends, I heard Lizzie say.

"Hi," a girl said from behind me. I whirled to find a short thing with big brown eyes and long black hair of about maybe twelve years old. "I'm Aniva, Amaal's daughter?"

"Oh, hi." I shook hands with Aniva.

"I liked your speech. I like your video, too. I've watched it like, a million times."

Wow. Someone out there actually liked my video. When I created it, my mother had made me disable comments, just so online trolls wouldn't have the chance to tear me down, because she knew I'd be affected by it, so I rarely got the chance to hear what people thought.

"I hope I can do that when I'm older," she said.

And then it hit me. I was an inspiration to someone, just like Lizzie had been to me. If I could help just one person, I'd done my job as a human being. I smiled widely at Aniva. "Thank you. You don't know what that means to me."

"Can I take a picture with you?" she asked.

"Sure."

She took a selfie with me then ran off blush-cheeked, while the other girls and I giggled. "Did that just happen?" Cassie asked.

"Julia, you're, like, a famous social media influencer," Tori said.

I smiled. Yep. I was.

"I'll see you guys at the gate." It was almost time to go, and I could feel that wave of sadness rising in my chest as it happened when something was about to end. I walked alongside my mom, dad, grandpa, and grandma, following Ms. Caroline to the Garden of Remembrance. "Where's Aunt Emma? Is she still being bombarded?" Everyone always wanted to shake her hand.

"You know how she is," my mom laughed. "We have to share her with others."

Suddenly, a rush of air joined us, followed by the men and woman in dark suits who kept watching over us at a distance. "Jules!" Aunt Emma gasped, out of breath. "I couldn't get away from the mobs. I've been trying to catch up to you. Hold still, chickadee."

"Yes, Madame President," I chuckled. I would never get used to seeing her as my Commander in Chief. To me, she would always be just...Aunt Emma. Lizzie's wonderful mom.

She held my shoulders still. "You're like a rock star, so elusive."

I blushed. No one was more rock star than my aunt, the President of the United States. "I saw you in the audience. Thank you for coming."

"I wouldn't have missed it. Not because...well, the obvious...but because I had to hear you speak. Believe it or not, I look up to you. I look at you and I see myself, or your mother, or your grandmother."

"Or you," I added.

She shrugged a *thank you.* "You've got it in you, Jules. You're going to do great things."

"Thank you," I said shyly. "I really do have a great family."

"Now, listen, I wanted to give you something." She broke me off from the group, took me aside near a potted palm. "I just came from Ms. Caroline's office where she gave me this." Aunt Emma opened her hand, producing a blue broken heart. A polymer clay half of a BEST FRIENDS charm. The half that said BE FRI. "Is this what you asked about at Lizzie's funeral?"

I almost couldn't breathe. "Yes. Where did you find it?"

"Apparently, it fell off her neck the day we left camp before the rally. A girl found it in the grass a while after Lizzie passed away and brought it to Ms. Caroline, saying it was Lizzie's because she'd seen her wear it."

"Oh." I placed my hand over my chest.

I was grateful to that girl, whoever she was. My eyes filled with tears again.

"Ms. Caroline said she didn't want to mail it to me, nor you, in case it would upset us, so she's kept it all this time. She asked if I wanted it, or if we should give it to you." Aunt Emma handed me Lizzie's heart, which launched me into a rollercoaster ride of emotions. "I said let's give it to you."

So, Lizzie *had* cherished the heart I'd made her. She hadn't taken it off like I'd thought—she'd only lost it.

"Thank you," I said, taking the little crude thing between my fingers.

I held it up to the sun and watched it sparkle. In it, I imagined Lizzie's smile. Slowly, I took mine out from my shirt and unfastened it from around my neck. Looping Lizzie's BE FRI half through, I put both halves of the heart together. *Best friends to the very end*. Everyone quieted as the sounds of families bubbled in the background, people saying goodbye, and exchanging contact info.

"Shall we go?" Aunt Emma led the way to the Garden of Remembrance.

Slowly, we walked through the beautiful space, taking in the butterflies, the colorful flowers and plants, the benches, pathways, even a little waterfall someone had added recently. I didn't know why I'd run that day Cassie and Tori had brought me in here. The place really was beautiful.

When we reached the statue of the little carefree girl running with the wind in her hair, we all paused to soak it in. The perfect work of art to capture Lizzie's spirit.

"I love it," Aunt Emma whispered, squeezing my hand and holding my mother's with her other. "This is really, truly special." We all gathered round to take group family photos with it.

"It really is," Mom agreed.

After all the group photos had been taken, I stared at the little girl. It may not have been the spitting image of Lizzie, but it definitely called forth her memory. All day, guests had been leaving flowers and teddy bears and American flags and photos of their daughters together with my cousin since arriving this morning. Our family hadn't brought anything since we'd already said goodbye to Lizzie two years ago. But I wanted to leave something behind, too.

The last time we'd ever been together was here in this spot, after all, before it was this beautiful place of remembrance.

Because you just never knew how long you'd live. You could be gone tomorrow. Or the next day. There was no point in holding onto painful things. *Closure*, I could hear Dr. Aileen in my mind. I slipped the cord from around my neck and stepped up onto the bench at the base of Lizzie's statue. Reaching up while my dad fussed about what I was doing, I laced the cord around the little girl's head. It settled onto her sculpted dress and sparkled in the sun.

There. Now Lizzie would always be able to wear it.

Behind me, Mom rested her hands on my shoulders, as I stared at the statue.

"See you next year for camp, beautiful girl." I

blew Lizzie a kiss.

Filtering out of the garden, we said our good-byes to all my mom and aunt's friends and to Ms. Caroline. "The great novelist, Julia Weissman," she said like she always did. I swore, I would never get tired of hearing that. She gave me a long hug that communicated a lot of unspoken words. "Thank you so much for standing up there today and saying all you did. Very powerful. I agreed with every word. I'll see you next year?"

"Yes." I nodded. "Maybe I can train to be a CIT. Or do I have to complete a whole year first?"

"We'll figure it out." Ms. Caroline gave me a warm smile. She glanced at my parents. "I bet you're feeling rather proud right about now."

"Julia makes us very proud." Mom glanced at me in that way moms do when all they see is the baby you were ages ago. "We've still have a long road ahead of us, Ms. Caroline. But…one day at a time."

"One day at a time," Ms. Caroline agreed then stepped back with a bow. "And now, if you'll excuse me, family, I have a few matters to take care of. Madame President, the honor has been mine."

"Oh, come here, Ms. C." Aunt Emma pulled Ms. Caroline into a hug.

I laughed. "Bye, Ms. Caroline. Love you."

She turned mid-hug to face me. "Love you, too, Julia. Promise me you'll help get your aunt re-elected in a few years."

"I promise."

I followed my parents to the Camp Auctus gates where families were saying goodbye and girls were throwing their green ribbons into the air. I took a few last-minute photos with Cassie and Tori, and even one with Tinay. We exchanged contact info. She said she had an idea for a new video, in case I wanted to do one with her. "Sure," I said and watched her leave, as she glanced back once to wave at me.

A black stretch limo waited for us with the engine running, surrounded by Secret Service agents. We all climbed in, as the crowd watched. My parents, aunt, and grandparents all quietly discussed how wonderful the mini reunion of friends was, while I stared out the window at the pine trees, the gravel trail, the scene I was leaving behind.

The welcome sign silently spoke to me:

Camp Auctus for Girls, Growing American Leaders Since 1801

"And I'm proud to be one of them," I whispered to myself. Proud to come from such a remarkable family. Proud to be a Camp Auctus sort-of alumni. Next year, I'd make it a full one. I almost couldn't wait.

"See you next summer," I whispered, lowering the window.

Once my family was finally settled, Aunt Emma gave the signal, and our driver slowly drove off through the gates. With my mom, aunt, and grandmother's smiling eyes on me expectantly, I remembered what to do. I reached up to my ponytail, plucked the green ribbon out of my hair, and tossed it into the wind.

JASON MILGRAM has loved both writing and computers since he was a child. At age eleven he won first place in an essay contest sponsored by National Geographic World, and started teaching himself computer programming.

Educated at the University of Cincinnati and MIT Sloan, Jason is currently a writer, a Vice President of Cloud Solutions at City National Bank of Florida, and a public speaker. He is also one of a couple of people in the United States to be awarded Microsoft's Azure MVP status every year since 2010.

Jason previously served in the US Army Reserve as a sergeant. He has also worked with the US Department of Justice and with leading technology companies such as IBM and Microsoft. An avid traveler he has been in almost every state of the United States, driven across the country multiple times, and visited sixteen countries. He currently lives in Cooper City, Florida with his wife and three dogs where he enjoys grilling several times a week.

A SUMMER REMEMBERED
(Book 2 – Council of Friends)

Releases October 4, 2020
Available for pre-order now.

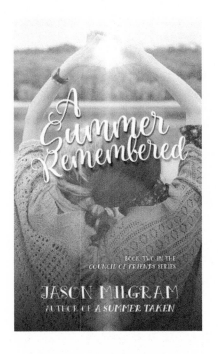

www.milgram.me